I Can ~~Only Dance~~ With You

She and Johnnie Dignam bumped into each other in Sauchiehall Street two days later. Maybe, as she went to work in the town and did her shopping in her lunch hour, she had been subconsciously keeping an eye open for him. Checking the faces above the multitude of uniforms for that shy half-smile and those light blue eyes. He knew her straight away and this time he asked her if she would like to go the pictures with him. That was the start. She had never had a serious boyfriend before. 'Picky and choosy,' Marie had called her. She had been waiting to fall properly in love, irrevocably and desperately, if you like, as in books and films, and now it had happened. Johnnie was it. Johnnie was going to be forever.

Jan Webster was educated at Hamilton Academy and worked as a journalist in Glasgow until she married fellow reporter Drew Webster and moved with him to London. Her stories have been published in Punch, many anthologies, and broadcast by the BBC, and her novels include the bestselling *Collies Row* and its sequel *Saturday City*, *Muckle Annie* and *I Can Only Dance With You*. She now lives in Macclesfield, Cheshire.

I Can Only Dance With You

Jan Webster

Woman's Weekly Fiction

A Woman's Weekly Paperback
I CAN ONLY DANCE WITH YOU

First published in Great Britain 1990
by Robert Hale Ltd
This edition published 1995
by Woman's Weekly
in association with Mandarin Paperbacks
an imprint of Reed Books Limited
Michelin House, 81 Fulham Road, London SW3 6RB
and Auckland, Melbourne, Singapore and Toronto

Copyright © Jan Webster 1990
The author has asserted her moral rights

A CIP catalogue record for this title
is available from the British Library
ISBN 1 86056 001 6

Printed and bound in Great Britain by
BPC Paperbacks Ltd
A member of
The British Printing Company Ltd

One

She was a pretty young woman, in the devastating, unknowing way some girls are at seventeen, before experience has left its stamp on them.

The cold crept into her shoes. They were hopeless shoes for a snowy night, anyhow, and had made her mother shake her head when she saw them, with their high heels, low vamp and butterfly bows on the instep. She stood underneath the station clock and stamped her feet repeatedly, but there was no feeling in her toes. Same went for her fingers, even inside the Ginger Rogers-type fur muff. It didn't look as if he was coming, and oh, God, she was going to cry. She had been waiting all day to see him, counting the minutes, so happy in her anticipation that she'd infected everyone in the Glasgow insurance office with a kind of mild hilarious gaiety. And now. She didn't know what to do now. They were supposed to be going dancing, meeting up with Rose at Green's Playhouse. What would she say to Rose if she had to turn up on her own? Even to your best friend it was hard to admit you had been stood up. But it was worse than that. She had never been in love before and she suspected that something deep and difficult and committed had happened to her and she did not want it getting out of control. She did not want to be upset because some man did not keep an assignation. But this was not just some man. This was Captain Johnnie

Dignam. And she had already given away great imaginative territories to him, in advance of any tenderness, beyond a kiss and a holding of hands. It was in her Calvinistic Scottish nature to find some way of blaming herself, but she honestly had not known what was happening to her. She had seen Johnnie Dignam and that had been it.

'Pardon me? Is it Helen Maclaren?' The slight figure in army uniform jolted her out of her frozen panic. In the station's gloom she could just make out a narrow, saturnine face with a half-pleading, half-defensive expression.

'Who are you?' she demanded.

'Johnnie Dignam's oppo. The name's Peter – Peter Hart. So sorry, he could not make it tonight. He asked me to send his apologies. I hope you haven't been waiting too long. Look, let's get you something to warm you up.' He took her elbow and began to lead her towards the station bar.

'I don't drink.'

'Coffee, then.'

She allowed him to place the coffee in front of her.

'Why couldn't he come?'

'Duties. You know how it is.'

'No, I don't. I've been standing there for ages, getting frozen.'

'Well, that was my fault. I took the wrong tram. Would you like to go to the pictures? With me?'

'We were supposed to be going dancing.' Her throat was rough with disappointment, but she was determined not to let this man see it. 'My friend is waiting for me at the Playhouse.'

'Then dancing we shall go. If you'll permit me to escort you.'

It was dark when the men straggled down Hope Street.

Sailing past them in the tram, her expression struggling from its mask of disappointment, Helen saw them in the moonlight and drew the attention of her companion to them. About a dozen men, wearing clothes that did not belong to them, cast-offs and knitted Balaclavas against the biting, snow-ridden wind, and carrying rough hapless bundles under their arms. The last man, young and fair-haired, carried a puppy. Helen had to look again to make sure she was seeing aright. Yes, a puppy it was and it looked as though the weary boy could scarcely hold the squirming yellow body.

She and Peter Hart exchanged surmising glances. 'Down in the Atlantic?' said Helen. 'Looks like they've been sunk, doesn't it?' But above their heads was a poster, of a man with his forefinger to his lips and the legend 'Careless Talk Costs Lives', and Peter Hart said reservedly 'Your guess is as good as mine.' But they both knew. The U-boats had been taking their toll. The straggling crocodile could not be anything else but survivors brought into the Clyde and safety and now on their way to their billets for the night. Helen gave herself a mental shake. These men had only just got away with their lives and here was she sunk in terminal gloom because Johnnie had been kept behind for unexpected duties. Truly, she abjured herself, it was time she grew up.

In the warmth and light of Green's Playhouse, after the blackout outside, her spirits rose a little. O.K. There was a war on. Soon she would be called up and have to go into the services or munitions. The bombers could be over any time. But there was this tacit acceptance that winning the war was about keeping up morale and you put the brutalities out of your mind whenever you could and danced and had a good time because that was what being young was about and you and the people you danced with might not be around forever to know what else there was about Life.

She hung up her muff, her little fur hat and the short fur cape, all of which she'd made from an old fur coat that had belonged to her grandmother. Everyone knew how to make things over these days and she saved her clothing coupons for things like the frivolous shoes and material for dresses. Underneath she wore a black crêpe de Chine dress with a sweetheart neckline decorated with two sparkling diamanté brooches. She fluffed out the reddy-gold hair that fell to her shoulders and lay in curly bangs above her forehead and adjusted the black velvet headband. The music of Oscar Rabin was making her feet twitch already.

'Rose, this is Captain Peter Hart. Johnnie couldn't come.' Rose Cassidy, black-haired and blue-eyed, saved from chocolate-box appeal by what Helen's mother called 'that hungered look' that came from being one of too big a family, and wearing an unsatisfactory skimpy blue crêpe dress and badly-fitting shoes gave Helen's companion a shrewd, assessing stare. 'How d'ye do?' she said shortly. Peter Hart gave a brief ironic bow.

A young lance-corporal with a very new, cropped haircut and spotty neck tapped Rose's elbow and asked her to dance. Peter Hart put his arm around Helen's narrow waist and led her into the music. 'Doesn't your friend have a partner – I mean, an escort?' he asked.

'You don't need a partner. She's with me,' said Helen boldly. Everybody went dancing, after all, and you didn't let lack of an initial partner stop you. The girls knew the rules and were armed by their innocence. But then Peter Hart spoke with the same kind of strangled drawl that Johnnie did and had probably gone to public school, too, and English public schoolboys were a lofty lot and didn't live like ordinary people. She was trying to understand them though. For Johnnie's sake she tried to break down Peter's reserve.

He really was being very considerate and polite, but

she hated it, just the same. He had no idea how patronising he sounded. Somehow with Johnnie it was different. There was something vulnerable about him that softened the unconscious upper-class arrogance, that made it seem more a foible than an attitude. He was so gentle and mannerly, so grateful for small everyday generosities like a cup of tea from her mother. In her mind she went over the miracle of their meeting – at a church dance, of all places, when with several other young officers he'd turned up halfway through the evening under the wing of the stuffy Sunday School superintendent. His battalion had just arrived in Glasgow and they were still coping with the local accents. She had gone to the dance with her sister Marie, who was home on leave from the WAAF.

She just loved dancing. Nearly all young Glasgow folk did and were good at it. He was a bit diffident when he asked her to partner him, but he was no slouch on the dance floor either. He looked down at her with delighted surprise. 'Hey, Ginger, where have you been all my life?' He acknowledged, as she did, the easy exuberance of their matched steps. Waltz, slow foxtrot, quickstep, 'Dashing White Sergeant', jitterbug – they tried them all. At the end of it, she was desperate for the lemonade he brought her, but filled with a dizzy, jubilant pleasure.

They did not make a date that evening. After he'd danced with her, he joined his fellow officers in a corner and did not even meet her eyes. She went home with Marie, thinking a bit about him, trying to sort out her impressions, but carefree and happy and unbothered because it had been a successful evening and Marie had had a good time, too. They fell into bed giggling and unmitigatedly cheerful.

She and Johnnie Dignam bumped into each other in Sauchiehall Street two days later. Maybe, as she went to work in the town and did her shopping in her lunch hour, she had been subconsciously keeping an eye open for him, checking the faces above the multitude of uniforms for that shy half-smile and those light blue eyes. He knew her straight away and this time he asked her if she would like to go to the pictures with him. That was the start. She had never had a serious boy friend before. 'Picky and choosy,' Marie had called her. She had been waiting to fall properly in love, irrevocably and desperately, if you like, as in books and films, and now it had happened. Johnnie was it. Johnnie was going to be forever.

She saw a grave, hesitant young man who looked almost too young to be in uniform – but then a lot of them did – and whose mood could change as they danced, responding to the impulse of movement, rhythm, music as though he couldn't have enough, as though they shut out darker things. He saw a fair-skinned, artless girl whose look of almost naked candour was the most noticeable thing about her; a girl with large, intelligent eyes and a body that made its own poetry out of the heroic amateurism of the orchestra.

They had locked into each other's mental processes with astonishing ease. Their quirks in humour were often identical. They both knew the words to the songs of Irving Berlin and they had both read Damon Runyon and O. Henry's story of the watch and the comb. He was surprised to hear her talk passable French with a Free French soldier introduced to them by the minister and she was amused at his surprise. She challenged him: 'Didn't you know about Scottish education? We always were ahead of the English,' refusing to be put down by his talk of Eton and Oxford.

'I don't think, d'you see, that it's going to work.' The waltz was slow and dreamy, you could move without thinking almost and Peter's face was drawn back from hers, and slightly sweating, and he was looking at her compassionately. They were about the same height, she thought, where Johnnie was taller, five foot eleven and a half, as he'd insisted, maybe even eleven and three quarters. She found Peter hard to categorise, from her inexperience, but four-square wasn't a bad description. Solid.

'What won't work?'

'What's between you and Johnnie. Whatever it is.'

She drew her hand away from his and removed his other hand from her waist, marching back towards the chairs and tables round the edge of the ballroom. She was glad to sit down because her legs were shaking.

'What do you mean?'

He sat down carefully beside her and slowly lit a cigarette from a silver cigarette case with his monogram on it.

'Helen, he should have told you. He's engaged. To someone out of the same kind of nest as he is. A rich man's daughter. Simonette. She's very nice. I know her. That's not to say you're not very nice, too. You are. But he's going to inherit a hell of a lot. Farms, a stately home, money. A publishing house. And that means responsibility. He can't do just as he likes. It ain't on, my dear. I'm sorry.'

'Why didn't he tell me himself? Surely –' He looked at her. She had gone an alarming white and he thought he heard her teeth chattering.

'I don't know his reasons. He's pretty mixed up.'

'Did he decide not to come tonight?'

'The colonel made it difficult for him. No, impossible. The colonel knows the situation. It's worried the hell out of him. He's a friend of Johnnie's father.'

'What's the matter with *me*?' She was amazed by her shaking anger. She was struggling, heartbreakingly as he saw it, for dignity. Her hands were clenched in her lap.

'He's already committed to Simonette. Oh, come on, Helen. You're going to have to take this on the chin. These things happen in wartime. Put it down to experience.'

'Oh, I won't let it get me down,' she assured him. Her chin went up, but he could see tears glittering in her eyes and when she shook her head one landed on his hand. It was as painful to him as a burn. 'I won't let my life depend to *that* extent on any man. But you can tell Johnnie Dignam this: I would have appreciated hearing all this from him, himself. Now, shall we dance?'

It was at that precise moment that Peter Hart, professional soldier not given to great depths of emotional insight, suddenly realised quite clearly what Johnnie Dignam saw in Helen Maclaren. A backbone which he, for all his charm and presence, did not yet possess.

Rose hated the dress. It had been her Auntie Kate's and then her mother had worn it twice and now she had fallen heir to it, but it was loose over her minimal bosom and the pearls from Woolworth's did nothing to improve matters.

Helen was dancing with the Captain and he must have said something to upset her because you could tell from her face. No doubt it had something to do with Johnnie. Goodness knows, Helen had made a big romance of it and she would be devastated if anything had happened. Rose was bursting with the need to know but she'd have to be patient. You couldn't just rush up to Helen and demand the full story. They weren't kids any more, though when they had been they'd babbled everything to each other. Rose being Catholic and Helen Protestant hadn't mattered a tin can to either of them.

When Frankie Aarensen from Chicago burst into the

ballroom with his shipmates, the skinny girl with the washed-out dress and the Minnie Mouse shoes was somehow the one his gaze kept landing on. There was something gentle and appealing about her, you knew she wouldn't be hard-boiled, so he sauntered over to her and took her hand in his. 'How about this one for me, kiddo?' he said.

He could dance. Rose could forgive him a lot, the bland assumption she would accept his invitation, the way his eyes slid past her face as though she wasn't there. But then she smelt it. The fear that came from young men who'd just come in from a bombing raid or an Atlantic convoy. The tension. 'You a Yank?' she demanded. 'You from up the street?' Further along Sauchiehall Street, the Beresford Hotel was now the headquarters for the American Red Cross. He'd obviously been kitted out there in some casual American civvies.

'Yeh, I'm a Yank,' said Frankie.

Rose took her partner over to the table where Helen and Peter were seated.

'I've seen you.' Helen gazed in amazement at the young man with the fair hair. 'You were carrying a puppy, a little yellow dog, down Hope Street. You looked as if –'

'Chap's probably been warned not to talk about it,' Peter intervened swiftly. 'All part and parcel of the war, eh? You been to Glasgow before?'

'First time.' Frankie looked at the British army officer gratefully.

'But the puppy,' Helen pursued. 'Did you rescue it? From the water? From the ship?' Frankie was shuffling his feet and Peter looked embarrassed. 'Oh, all right,' she gave in. 'I know. "Be like Dad – keep Mum." I'm sorry I asked.'

The band struck up a lively tango and Frankie took Rose back into the dancing crowd.

'Are you up to this?' asked Rose bluntly. She could feel a desperate tired hysteria communicate itself to her body from his, a trembling and a need to talk, to be comforted.

'Just dance, kiddo,' he pleaded. Rose danced. She twirled the shabby dress around her slender hips as though she were Betty Grable, she matched her feet in her cousin's borrowed shoes to Frankie's nimble ones in their two-toned brogues.

There was laughter all around them, the lights in the ballroom were bright and warm, the girls' dresses swirled like the petals of flowers. They were safe and contained in the moment, all anyone could expect. It was the reason Frankie Aarensen had come here, resisting the M.O.'s advice to rest after what had happened to his ship.

'You were crazy going back for a dog,' the doctor had said. Frankie had said nothing. You couldn't explain without making yourself some kind of hero.

'You wanna be my girl?' asked Frankie Aarensen. The words had risen up unbidden.

Rose laughed, executing a complicated jitterbug step in her cousin's big best shoes. 'I've only just met you.'

'But we kinda get along, don't we?' Frankie insisted. 'You like me, don't you?'

'How do I know whether I like you yet or not?'

'I know I like you. You're pretty.'

Rose went a bright pink.

'I got nylons. You interested in nylons?'

'Depends.'

'Depends on what?'

'You know.' Some girls went much too far, much too quickly, in their anxiety to acquire nylon stockings. She wanted Frankie to know she wasn't one of them.

Frankie looked at her, grinned and pulled her to him.

'No strings,' he assured her. 'I only like classy dames. You're a classy dame.' It was strange, he thought, how fast the glassy deep waters of the Atlantic, the cold and the terror, going back for the ship's pup because he had heard its terrified yelping, how fast all that evaporated when you held a girl in your arms. Like you were secure. Like the fuzz on a girl's forearms, the way her soft mouth quirked under its bright lipstick, the way she looked at you, had a special power to make everything safe and good and possible.

Rose looked across at Helen. She and Peter Hart were sitting as though part of a tableau, stiff and uncomfortable and uncommunicative.

Oh Lord, she thought, she's got that Sunday-go-to-meeting expression. Rose had never been one for getting above herself, as her mother put it. Living from hand to mouth, as the Cassidy family did, you couldn't afford to.

But Proddies were different. Helen was different. Helen had a terrible stiff pride that was a very Proddie thing and that you wounded at your peril. Over the years Rose had learned to respect it. Helen was sitting there, stitching her pride together, and Rose felt a terrible rush of protective pity for her friend.

Two

The girls used the same close mouth, that is to say the same entrance to their parents' ground-floor tenement flats. The close was tiled with cold white and black checked tiles and washed out regularly with strong disinfectant, so that the smell hit your nostrils the minute you entered. A baffle wall had been built to counteract blast during air-raids. Often total strangers necked at the far dark corner or on the landings on the way to the upper apartments. The building was badly in need of up-dating but the war had stopped all that. It was pervaded, however, with a new sense of prosperity that had come with the war and full employment for the tenement dwellers – even women who had not worked since marriage were making good money in munitions and elsewhere.

They had walked home arm in arm after getting off the tram from Sauchiehall Street, refusing to be escorted by either Frankie Aarensen or Peter Hart. There was solid sorority between them.

'What shall I tell Johnnie, then?' Peter Hart had asked Helen, eventually.

'What is there to tell him?' she had replied, in bewilderment. How could she express her pain and wounded dignity? She had been brought up to be a proud girl, proud of her religion, her Scottishness, her family and their sense of decency, that fact they had never owed anybody anything and paid their rent on time and that she had won a bursary to a good school. 'I can hold my head up wherever I go,' was her mother's creed and only the children knew what this cost her sometimes. She could not see that money made any difference to a person's worth, but Peter Hart – and Johnnie Dignam – evidently thought so.

'You could tell him you understand,' said Peter Hart, with an intense probing look.

'I don't,' she informed him. 'But I'll survive.' He could only admire the way she fought to pretend nothing untoward had happened, but the sight of her poor little pinched face would stay with him for a long time.

'Come in to our place for a cup of tea?' Rose suggested.

'I'll just tell Mammie I'm back first,' Helen answered.

Her mother was nodding by the fire over a copy of the *People's Friend*. Her father, Willie, having had a few drinks, was already in bed. The weekly rations would have been bought and put away. Even now, with her other children in the armed forces and what you could buy severely curtailed, her mother enjoyed shopping and the feeling of money in her purse. The flat emanated a kind of Friday-night contentment and even if it was reluctantly, Jessie Maclaren gave her consent to Helen going next door. Custom and the war had worn down what religious bigotry might have existed between the two families at the start. Jessie Maclaren lent out her fox fur and jet beads to Kate Cassidy for weddings and funerals and Kate Cassidy was the only woman Jessie Maclaren would honour by borrowing a cup of sugar from because, she explained, she gave with a generous heart. (Protestant friends would have regarded borrowing as feckless.)

'I'm away to my bed,' said Jessie, adding in admonition, because her daughter looked a bit pale-faced, 'and don't you be too long, even if it is Saturday tomorrow.'

The Cassidy flat was always well occupied, with visiting relatives as well as members of the family. Joe Cassidy, the father, was snoozing in his chair before the grate, the toes sticking out of his ancient slippers, while Kate prepared vegetables for the next day while topping up the teacup of her cousin Annie and comforting her about her latest pregnancy. ('Sure now, Annie, they bring their own love with them.') Rose's younger sister, Bernadette, who was 'delicate', had her head in a pulp magazine. Helen always thought of her as being 'elsewhere'. She was fey and dedicated to being good. Helen and Rose could not retreat to the front room for youthful Cassidys were already bedded down there, in the fold-up bed, but over a corner of the big untidy table Helen at last poured out some of her hurt to her friend.

'So who does he think he is?' demanded Rose, with passionate ire.

'Too good for me, it seems,' said Helen.

'Nobody's too good for you,' insisted Rose loyally. 'Sure you've got Highers, you could have been a teacher if you'd wanted. And look at the books you read. Our Brendan thinks the world of you. Of your brain, I mean – your mind,' Rose amended hastily. She saw her eldest brother as a kind of secular priest and above liking any girls in *that* way. Sure they'd tried to get him into the priesthood, but he wasn't that way inclined.

Brendan raised his head from the book he was reading and gave them a lazy smile.

'What are you two on about?'

'Nothing,' said Rose. 'Private matters.'

Brendan smiled at Helen, an engaging, understanding smile which showed he had overheard perfectly well what the girls were talking about. He closed his book

deliberately and moved his chair nearer them. To
Helen he said, 'You coming to night school Monday
night?' They were both studying public speaking. In
Helen's case, she did not know why, except that it was all
part of learning to do things. Brendan was clear. He
wanted to be a councillor and then maybe even an M.P.
Excused National Service because of a mild heart
condition, he was already a shop steward in the factory
where he worked. In the chaotic and often volatile
family he stood out like some figure out of rock, solid,
studious, a kind of working-class aristocrat, wise well
beyond his years. He was also darkly good-looking in a
brooding, introspective, defensive kind of way. Helen
liked him inordinately. He passed all her tests of good
manners and common sense and was nearly always
good-humoured and kind. At twenty-five, she had till
recently regarded him as practically middle-aged,
although now nearing eighteen herself, she began to see
he might not totally have gone over the edge towards
the sere and yellow.

In the public-speaking class, he was a far better orator
than the rest of them, vivid and passionate and so witty
you hated it when he sat down. Helen loved putting
words in order, too, and had a feeling for them, but
when she was on her feet all her inhibitions seemed to
surface and she blushed, shuffled and did not always
give her ideas their head.

In answer to Brendan's question now she said 'I
might not feel like it.' She knew that on Monday night
and a lot of other nights she would want a corner to
herself, where she could perhaps weep in private. And
fight this great, bruising hurt that was growing, not
fading, inside her.

He did a surprising thing then. He put out a hand
and touched her arm. 'You come,' he said, and it was an
order. His eyes always did that to you – invited you to

take up arms and go out there and fight whatever devils needed fighting. She felt response rise in her. 'O.K. Brendan,' she acquiesced, to Rose's delight. 'I'll be there.'

'Attagirl,' he said.

'And what about joining the Labour Party?' Brendan had urged, as they walked home after the night class, arguing about this and that as they always did.

'I don't know.' She was interested, fascinated, by all the talk about what kind of country they were going to have after the war, but politics wasn't the road she wanted to go down.

'We'll have to have a fairer society,' he insisted. 'People who've been in the war aren't going to settle for slums and unemployment after it.'

It was funny, really, how they stopped every time at their respective doors on either side of the close, like something out of a stage set. Often they were still talking as they let themselves in and their goodnights were swallowed up in the long lobbies. Tonight he came to her door, took the key from her cold hands and fumbled to engage it. That done, he did not turn the key.

'You've been miles away,' he chided.

'I know. I'm a bit tired.'

'You've got a lot in front of you. Do you know that? A whole world, full of excitement, books, art –'

It was so dark in the blacked-out close, she had to strain to make out his face, but she sensed he was looking at her with a new kind of intensity, almost pleading with her to share her misery with him, let him help.

'I know that, Brendan,' she said, with her almost stately seriousness.

'Well then.'

She knew something else. She knew he wanted to kiss

her. But she was very far from being involved with him on any kind of emotional level. Light years away from him, almost pitying him because he had never known the highs and lows that she had over these last few weeks. Deftly she turned the key and was gone before his soft reluctant goodnight thudded against the faded paint of the battered front door.

'Do you want to come skating with Frankie and me?' Rose demanded. These days, it was Frankie this and Frankie that. Rose was being showered with nylons, scented soap and bars of chocolate, spoiled with best seats at the pictures and meals out. Except that nothing could spoil Rose, who shared Frankie's largesse with her appreciative family and friends.

The girls had met for lunch at one of the new serve-yourself places that had sprung up since hostilities began.

'No thanks,' said Helen. 'You deserve to have Frankie all to yourself. He won't be here forever.'

Big ready tears sprang to Rosie's eyes. 'I don't want him to go away,' she said, swallowing sobs and hot soup simultaneously and hiccupping in the process. 'He might – he might not be so lucky the next time.'

'He will be,' said Helen. Frankie was such a positive, physical presence there was no way, she felt, U-boats or any other danger were going to remove him.

'I light candles for him,' said Rose, cheering slightly.

'The war's going to be over soon, anyway.'

'I'm going to Chicago then.'

'To marry him? Has he asked you?'

'He doesn't need to. I'm just going to be with him, wherever he is.'

'Watch out, Rosie. Don't lose your head –'

'Listen to who's talking!' said Rosie.

'What about the puppy?'

'When it comes out of quarantine, I'm going to take care of it. I'm calling it Sam – after Uncle Sam.'

Helen supposed that indicated a certain genuine commitment on Frankie's part. He wouldn't entrust the puppy he'd risked his life for to just anyone. She was impressed.

The afternoon closed down dark and cold in the insurance office where Helen filed relentlessly. She did the work conscientiously enough, but it didn't engage her. She was beginning to sense what people meant when they talked about careers. She would have to put her mind to it: to what she was going to become. Not just a cog, not just an adjutant. But something in her own right. Only Brendan had seen the true necessity of this and tried to guide her in the courses open to her. At one time a teaching or a nursing career were seen as the pinnacles a girl from her background should aspire to – but the war had changed all that, mixed up everybody's aspirations.

Should she admit, even to herself, that what she really saw herself doing was being a reporter? It sounded very upstart and outlandish, but today, feeling low, she needed the prod of ambition. Without telling anyone, she had written to the editors of various Glasgow papers, enquiring about her chances, and had received discouraging replies, except from one who told her to learn shorthand and typing and then write again. She had been taking shorthand and typing at night school, anyhow, along with the public-speaking class, with a view to improving her prospects in the insurance office. Her boss had hinted that in the New Year there was the possibility of promotion. But how high could she rise? The upper echelons were a solid wall of men.

And there was the other matter she saw as being part of her education, her preparation for The Rest of her Life. She had to cope with the matter of loving a man.

Not as her mother did, scolding, shielding, upbraiding her father. Not like Rose with Frankie, which seemed to involve an immense amount of gratitude for the gifts admittedly showered. But opening up, giving and sharing with a soul-mate was how she had seen it. The way it had been with Johnnie. She wasn't getting that sorted out at all and she was a practical girl who hated not finding answers. She could read and understand Ibsen and Goethe, she rattled through Hemingway like a train, her schoolwork had never been a burden to her, but she had no idea how to find her way back to some kind of equilibrium after what had happened over Johnnie.

She went home after work but, restless and dissatisfied, decided to do an extra stint at the forces canteen in Renfield Street, as she had half-promised the supervisor. The work was mainly making omelettes from dried eggs, or toasting buns, for the young soldiers, sailors and airmen who crowded in off trains or buses or Service vehicles.

Of course they wanted to flirt with you. It didn't hurt to be nice to them, unless they got serious and pestered you for a date, but you could see that coming and the girls all knew how to deal with it. It was a very busy night. She made omelettes till the arm that flicked them over ached and at ten o'clock she put on her coat and went to catch her tram home.

A figure loomed in front of her as she stepped out on to the street. A figure brandishing something in the blackout, a sweet-scented something that could only be roses. 'Your mother said you'd be here,' said Johnnie Dignam.

She began to walk away, but the scent of roses lingered near her, and followed her on to the tram. Johnnie Dignam sat down beside her. A cold wind ran through the big, draughty vehicle from front to back and its various mechanisms clanked and whirred over the rain beating viciously on the windows.

'A typical Glasgow night,' offered Johnnie Dignam.

'If you don't like it, stay away.' How hard it was, not to look at his pale blue hypnotic eyes.

'I may have no choice.'

'And what does that mean?' She looked at him directly for the first time.

'Simply that. I had to see you before – before *then*. Please take these.' She refused once again.

They got off the tram and he held her elbow lightly as they crossed the road. (Oh, the treachery of elbows!)

'Would your parents let us have the use of the front room?'

'Whatever for?'

'To talk. Just to talk. Please, Helen.'

She let him follow her in the door. When her mother heard voices and came questioningly into the lobby, Helen said, 'It's him. Johnnie. Can we go in the front room for a wee while, Mum? Please.'

Jessie Maclaren nodded bemusedly, but she was no stranger to young people and their emotional upsets and she supposed there was a war on. Even to young men who might break her daughter's heart she could not be wholly inhospitable. It went against the Glasgow grain.

'Go on, then,' she relented. 'And you can put on one bar of the fire.'

The light was bright and revealing after the murky dark of the blacked-out streets. From the moquette suite came a delicate whiff of mustiness. 'Sit down,' said Helen brusquely. He looked down at his hands.

'Two more days,' he said, like an incantation. 'I've got two more days. I had to see you. Even if it's only to explain.'

She could have said angrily, 'Explain what?' but she

knew very well and could scarcely bear to hear it, so she said nothing. He fumbled in the pocket of his jacket and brought out an envelope with a photograph inside, handing it to her portentously. It was of a huge house, bigger and grander and whiter than anything she had ever seen in her life.

'It's Knoleberry Park,' he said. 'Which I stand to inherit.'

'So?' she demanded stonily.

'Simonette's money is supposed to shore it up.'

'And you go along with such things?' She had never heard herself sound so stony-hearted.

'That's simply the situation. It's awfully complicated, because of my father. And then I came here and fell in love with you. I've been so wanting to tell you. I just want *you*, Helen. What are we going to do?'

It was no use. He had used the word love. She could not keep him away any longer. She looked at him with all her longing and he leapt across the small space between the two chairs, taking her in his arms and kissing her with a wild fervour. Her lips fell open, her body sagged in abandonment, everything in her responded with an incredible relief and joy. Tears fell as heedlessly as Niagara.

'You should have come,' she whispered. 'The other night. You should not have let them stop you. You should have come and told me everything yourself.'

'I would have been on a charge. It was physically impossible. I think the C.O. would have chucked me in jankers.'

She said, very positively, from the depths of her own determined nature, 'Johnnie, nobody can make you do something you don't want to do.'

He took her hands, pressed them together and kissed them. Then with a smile that didn't quite come off he moved away from her.

'You don't know my father. The inheritance means everything to him. He came out of the last war, half-blinded, a leg shot away and the place – Knoleberry Park – in hock because of *his* father's debts. He pulled it all together for me.'

'He put it all on your shoulders?'

'You could put it like that.'

'And you want it?'

'It isn't a question of wanting. It's family duty. There *is* only me.'

'And where does Simonette come in? Are you really thinking of marrying her just for her money?'

'Of course not. What do you take me for? She likes the idea of being mistress of an estate, of having an old family name and all that goes with it. Her father's quite open about the money she'll bring. He's a bit of an old Philistine. Being accepted really matters to him.'

She looked at him helplessly. 'Johnnie,' she said, 'none of this makes any sense to me. I can't connect what you're talking about with the person in front of me.' She looked at him almost clinically. He was very slender, patrician, with his fine, long hands, straight nose, wide brows and gently waving fair hair. Totally, totally different from the sturdy, straightforward working-class Scots she'd grown up with, who fought authoritarian fathers for their independence.

'What about your mother?' she demanded curiously.

'She's a bolter.'

'What does that mean?'

A gentle pink ran up under his fair skin. She said quickly, 'I don't mean to pry, for goodness' sake.'

'She ran off with a bounder from the local hunt.'

'Do you see her?'

'From time to time,' he said distantly. He jumped up, as if wishing to distance himself from the subject. 'Helen,' he demanded, passionately, 'we've so little time, let's talk about *us*. Things'll work out, somehow. But let's have a pact that the next two days belong to us.' He pulled her down on to his knee and traced her mouth and eyes with his forefinger. 'I can't get you out of my mind. It's as though when I confront you, I confront another part of myself. I never knew it before, but love is hell, if you can't be with – with the other person. I kept thinking of how we danced together, that first night we met. Dancing's the nearest you get to being one person, apart from – well, you know what I mean.'

He kissed her. She knew that any moment her mother would tap tactfully on the door and suggest that it was time Johnnie was away for his tram, but even as she listened she was going out to meet him wherever it was he wanted her. Her mind was trying to sort out its confusions but the rest of her was in a kind of mad ecstasy that was part physical, part spiritual.

She knew exactly what he meant about the attraction between them. Something magical had happened which meant that all their defences were down. They knew each other – had done from the start – in a way that was confounding and wonderful. There would be little things to know about him – his tastes, what made him laugh – but what he was, essentially, she already knew. Already she loved him. That was incontrovertible. That was something war and its desperation did to you. You had to make pacts before you were ready for them.

Three

'Where do you think they will send you?' asked Helen. Of course if he had an inkling he wasn't allowed to tell her. But they speculated. It could be the Middle East, it could be Italy, it could even be the Far East. Or maybe – and everybody's mind was full of it – this was going to be the Second Front, the final assault on Europe, that would finish Hitler off and that would be desperate and bloody above anything that had gone before.

'Why should you go?' she demanded, with passionate entreaty. 'You didn't make this war. Look what the last one did to your father – and mine. Mine won't even talk about it. After all this time he can't face the filth and evil of it. Why aren't we all pacifists? We will pay a terrible price for what we've done before God.'

'What about the death camps? The people who are too helpless to help themselves? Hitler is the evil, Helen. After we've sorted him out, we can start again.'

She clung to him then. They were walking about in the rain, that first of the last two days, only half aware of what was going on around them. Stopping to look into each other's eyes, to try and read – what? The future? The explanation of what was happening to them? People walked around them, respecting their privacy. They weren't such a rarity, people troubled by love, people cramming everything they could into brief leaves, brief liaisons. *There's a war on.* It took a war to

heighten and define what life was all about. Everybody
knew that. Then.

He bought her a ring. A signet ring for her right hand.
She would not even contemplate any other sort, while he
was still tied up with Simonette. He bought her flowers.
Her mother sighed when she took the armful home and
arranged them in every available vase or jug.

They went dancing, moving round the Plaza in Glasgow's south side like sleep-walkers, the violinist Benny
Loban mingling with the dancers, bowing to their
applause. For a little while, the strange wartime panacea
of the dance comforted and consoled them.

One more day to go. They would like to have spent the
night together. He wanted to sleep with her. He wanted
to fall asleep with her beside him, and wake up with her
beside him. There was no way it could happen.

They were given courtesy of the Maclaren front room
until as late as they wanted. It could not be too late
because he had to get back to the barracks. In a fumbling,
unsatisfactory way he attempted to take her virginity.
She wept and he wept. The next day they met early and
went to a cinema. After that, it did not much matter
where they went, because he was leaving her. They went
into a broken-down, rain-sodden telephone booth for
one last embrace, out of the weather. Then she saw him
walk away through a dark and crumbling railway bridge,
over cobbles, not turning to wave until the very last, till he
was almost gone from her sight and ken.

She had an insane desire to run after him, to upset all
the crazy edifice of the war, to stop every single plane or
ship leaving British shores. But in the end, he had
wanted to go. He believed in the war. And somehow she
found the strength to walk home through the inhospitable night, pretending normality, even stopping at shop
windows, though she took nothing in.

She met Brendan Cassidy in the close, going out as she

was coming in.

'A rotten night, Helen,' he greeted her. She stared at him, as though he had said something in Swahili. 'Hello Brendan,' she said. He thought the weather had chilled her to the marrow and did not detain her. He turned his own collar up as he dived into the rain and wind.

'You heard from lover-boy yet?' On the nights she walked home from the public-speaking class with Brendan Cassidy he always asked her the same question. And still the answer was no. She did not know whether Johnnie was alive or dead, well or wounded, in Europe or North Africa or Burma. Brendan Cassidy could only pity her – she was so young and so vulnerable and Service mail so unpredictable. But some niggling demon he'd not been able to stamp out made him try and talk her out of such deep commitment to the Englishman they both knew was still formally committed to somebody else.

'You're too young anyhow,' he half joked. 'You don't want to be taking any man seriously at your age.'

'What would you know about it?' she replied patiently. As far as she knew, all Brendan's commitments – certainly his financial ones – were to his hard-up family and needed more than ever now with Bernadette, the one just under Rose in age, sick with tuberculosis of the spine, and confined to a sanatorium in Lanarkshire.

Stung for once out of his lofty, if assumed, equanimity, Brendan replied, 'I've had my moments.'

'Who with?' she demanded ungraciously and ungrammatically.

'Just let's say – I've been attracted. For example, I'm attracted in a way to you.'

She laughed, bumping into him in the blackout, sounding her age for once.

'A fine pair we'd make. What would our parents say?'

'You mean the religious thing? I'm a believer in Marxist dialectics, Helen. I haven't been near a church for years.'

'I would rather you were a Catholic than a Communist, Brendan.'

'I want to improve matters here, down here, not wait till we're Up There.'

There was an almost companionable silence while she digested this offering.

'Maybe the war has brought Christians together, anyhow,' she said. 'My Dad used to be a Wee Free – he thought the Pope, pardon me for saying this in front of you, was the Anti-Christ. Now he thinks it's Hitler.'

'Why can't you come out with me, just for one night?' The question was out before he'd had time to consider it.

'I don't think so, Brendan. Thanks anyhow.'

'You just have a crush, you know. Every woman carries this daft torch for the first man she's slept with.'

'I didn't sleep with him,' she protested. 'Not that I wouldn't have done –'

'There is the possibility you'll never hear from him again.' It was out, the cruelty he could not contain. He wasn't in control of himself at all. Had that really been his voice with the bitter jibing note to it?

'I think I'll walk home from the class on my own in future, Brendan,' she said, stiffly.

'Don't be daft. In the blackout?'

'So what?'

'I'm sorry. I just don't feel we're the friends we used to be –'

'Whose fault is that?'

'Mine, I suppose,' he admitted humbly. 'Look, if I lend you my book on Freud, we can talk about that instead of other things that upset you. What do you say?'

'O.K.' she agreed. At the doors to their homes they shook hands on it, grinning in the dark.

'What's up, Rosie?' Frankie Aarensen demanded, his young face pink with concern. They had taken the tram to the south side of the city, to Linn Park, and were walking with their arms twined round each other's waists. They went everywhere like that, drooping like flowers when they were separated. They knew it could not be long now till he had to join his new ship.

'Bernadette, of course.' Rose wasn't vain in the way other girls Frankie knew were vain. She didn't dab her eyes gently and worry about them getting swollen and red and unsightly. When she wept she wept, the tears soaking her cheeks and the thick network of black lashes. Conversely, because she was so unmanipulative, it brought it out this permanent protective tenderness in him. 'Don't,' he pleaded, his arm tightening around her.

'She's so sick, Frankie. We're going to lose her.'

'You don't know that.'

'I know from looking at my mother. It's pulling the life out of her too.'

'Try not to cry, Rosie. I don't want to think of you like this when I go away. You're going to have to be tough and brave.'

With a mighty indrawing of breath she tried to quell her tears.

'Nothing's got to happen to *you*,' she warned.

'Nothing will.'

They sat down on one of the park seats. It struck cold up through their bodies. They clung to each other and their lips met. Roller-skating children went past them, taking their heedless embrace for granted.

'You'll like Chicago,' he said presently. 'You know it's on a lake? It gets cold there, too, as cold as Scotland. I'm going to make it big there, Rosie. Have my own plant.

Refrigeration. Meat. And a house with an apple orchard and a horse and dogs.'

'And kids.'

'You can have as many as you like,' he said accommodatingly.

'It isn't true.' She pushed him away suddenly and looked at him with a gut-wrenching, desolate expression. 'It's all just talk between me and you, isn't it? It's what happens at the pictures. I'll never get to Chicago. Who am I kidding?'

'If I say you will, you will.' His young voice broke protestingly. 'I'm not talking day-dreams, Rosie. I mean what I say.'

She said, in a low, forsaken voice, 'You don't get what you want. You get what's sent you. I'll need to stay here, if Bernadette – if Bernadette –' She could not finish that particular sentence. 'We're *poor*,' she protested. 'They need what I earn. The house gets too much for my mother and I have to help her.'

'But you'll be making a new life for yourself. That's your entitlement.'

'I don't see it that way. If we're talking entitlement, what's Bernadette's? She's been good all her days, she never fights, she's the best that ever was. Fifteen years on this earth – where's the entitlement there?'

'Don't talk like that,' he said sombrely. 'We could all talk like that. I had a pal and I saw him dive off the ship and hit the lifeboat bow and sink like a stone.' He shouldn't be talking about it but he couldn't help it, this once. 'I went back to get the dog, to get Sam, because it was saving *something*, it wasn't even brave, I was too mixed up, but it was better than nothing. It wasn't Robbie, though. I could do nothing for him, and he was my friend, he liked Nellie Lutcher and molasses on his bread and he had the longest toes I ever saw on a man, they stuck through every pair of socks he ever had.'

Now it was her turn to plead. 'Don't,' she said and they moved close together again and began eventually to talk of lighter things, why her hands were so much smaller than his, and how he could bend his thumb back to his wrist and their chances of catching high tea at the Ca'doro if they hurried back to town.

Jessie Maclaren knew the knock at her front door. It was how Kate Cassidy knocked when she had the need to borrow something – timidly, apologetically, a sad little rallentando fading away to nothing. She opened the door quickly to save her neighbour prolonging the agony.

'Kate! Come in.'

Kate stepped into the lobby, bringing something of the crowded family life lived across the passage with her – cooking odours, slight gaseous sensations from the fire she had just kindled and a lap dampened recently by a visiting baby. Her once dark hair was greying and her plump figure was shapeless and dishevelled, but she moved on dainty feet, lightly, like a dancer. Her face was bloated from crying and her voice thick.

'Jessie, is there an old coat you could be letting me have?' Kate's hands twisted nervously, endlessly. 'I wouldn't be after asking, but they've just been up from the paper shop with a telephone call from the hospital and Bernadette's been took right bad.'

Jessie had the lobby press open before the sentence was finished and she was helping Kate into the navy coat she had just started to wear for shopping. Automatically she reached into her pinny pocket for a clean hankie to dab uselessly at Kate's streaming face.

'I lent my coat to our Theresa after hers got soaked,' Kate was babbling. 'I wouldn't be troubling you, Jessie, but they're all out.'

Jessie unhooked her own raincoat from inside the lobby press. 'I'll come with you,' she said, decisively. 'I'll just leave a note on the table.' She picked up her leather purse from the kitchen dresser, in case Kate did not have the price of their tram fares, her mind dark with foreboding. The little girl who had always been ready to run a message for her if her own children were absent, the one with the big appealing eyes, could she really be slipping away so soon to join the Catholic saints Jessie knew so little about?

All she could remember was Bernadette in a washed-out print frock that had belonged to her own Helen, dancing at a backyard concert for the troops, or setting off for mass in a straw bonnet bought with her father's racing winnings, a tidemark on her thin little neck where the face flannel hadn't landed. She dashed her own tears away angrily. It was no contest, was it, a child reared on bread and marge and promises and this random disease that dipped and claimed in the tenements? Unselfconsciously, she held Kate's hand all the way to the hospital.

'I'm sorry, Mrs Cassidy,' said the ward sister. 'I'm afraid it's bad news. There was a sudden turn for the worse this morning. We couldn't do anything for her.'

A young priest came red-faced towards them, holding out his hands.

'She had the Last Rites,' he said to Kate. 'I got here in time. She went like one of the saints to her Maker.'

Jessie's hands went out towards her neighbour.

'Thanks, Father,' said Kate automatically. 'Sure you've been good all the way along.'

'Do you want to see her?' asked the sister.

They stood one on either side of the tiny frail body. Kate touched her child's hand and chest and kissed her brow. She did not want to leave her. At last Jessie walked round to her and drew her gently away.

'We'll go home now,' she said. 'Your other bairns are waiting for you, Katie.'

'The bastards,' said Kate Cassidy. 'They took my bairn away from me and what harm had she ever done? No, no, Jessie. Don't let them take her away.'

What bastards, thought Jessie Maclaren. Poverty? Fertility? Fecklessness? Where could you lay the blame?

They all said how well Kate Cassidy had stood up to the funeral. 'She has the comfort of her faith,' said her cousin Annie. She wouldn't even let them make so much as a cup of tea – she herself had to do it, had to make sure Father Bailey got a piece of sultana cake, that her youngest had a clean hankie and did not let her nose run. Maybe she had the comfort of knowing Bernadette was with the two little brothers who had died in infancy. Sure she was a brave woman, just the same.

One morning Kate Cassidy got up and put round her shoulders the plaid shawl that until the war many women had worn as a kind of badge of maternal servitude.

She went to mass then took a tram to the Cowcaddens where she had been born and where she and Joe had started their married life. The sister she had intended to visit was out but by this time it did not matter to her. She was walking the streets with the tears riding unbidden down her cheeks. Onlookers said she walked deliberately in front of the big Clydesdale horses pulling scarce precious coal for Cowcaddens fires. Certainly when the bobby tried to pull her away she fought and struggled with him, calling him dreadful names, scratching at his face like a demented thing. They put her in a police cell, as much to calm her as anything, and the next morning, following a pale-faced prostitute into the dock, she was charged at the police court with attempted suicide, before her case was dismissed.

The doctors said she would not be able to return to her family for quite some time. She needed rest and care. Perhaps it was the right decision. Jessie Maclaren was not surprised by any of it. She had seen the light go out of Kate's face the minute the priest came towards them, that day in the hospital.

Four

It was a glorious early autumn day and they had taken a picnic to the banks of the Clyde. At least, Helen had brought the picnic, which consisted of stale but precious cheese grated on to white bread and a flask of tea, some reasonable apples and chocolate bought with the last of her sweet coupons. The war might be over but there was no sign of rationing relaxing its squeeze. She had insisted that Rose should save any delicacies that might otherwise have been contributed to the picnic for their visit to Kate Cassidy in the convalescent home.

They were quiet as they self-consciously spread the faded travelling rug on the dried-out grass. Brendan had invited himself along at the last minute and was now demurring about taking a sandwich.

'There's enough,' Helen urged. She was not all that keen on cheese anyhow and her appetite had been blunted by arguments with her father before she set out.

'You're seeing far too much of those Cassidys,' he'd argued. 'Can you no' find somebody who kicks wi' the same foot as you do?' He meant of the same religious persuasion. But of course it was useless to get into arguments with her dad over such things, to try and tell him war had swept away the old prejudices. It had been bad enough trying to convince him the sky wouldn't fall in when last month the country had decided they didn't

39

want Churchill any more and Clement Attlee had come in instead to head a Labour government. Her dad was a stubborn Tory of the old school who had nothing but contempt for shop stewards and union leaders like Brendan, whom he saw as taking away a man's independence and ability to stand on his own two feet. (The fact that his own two feet often took an unsteady path from the pub on the corner was something he conveniently ignored.)

There was something else. She had something to tell them, something it was important they heard from her rather than gossiping neighbours in the tenement. She kept waiting for the right moment.

Rose and Brendan had been subdued by the sight of their mother. A preternaturally clean, scrubbed and shrunken Kate was now in the care of the nuns at the convalescent home, obeying their gentle daily strictures with the submission of a meek child and praying in the chapel for the souls of her lost babies. Of the spirit that had once rattled Joe Cassidy out of his chair to go look for work and rallied her brood for Sunday mass there was no sign. Neither Rose nor Brendan thought their mother would ever come back to them as she had once been. Brendan's thoughts were even blacker, for he had had a long talk with the doctor about his parent's loss of the will to live and the medico had not sounded at all hopeful, especially as Kate had a history of complications arising from her many pregnancies.

But what was affecting them most, what they had been talking about all the way from the convalescent home, were the atom bombs on Hiroshima and Nagasaki. The first one had been bad enough, but the second one – dropped only this week – where was the moral justification for it?

'If it saves any more loss of life, then it's been worth it,' Rose argued. But like the other two, she was stunned by the sense of guilt the bombing had engendered in her. They could scarcely look into each other's eyes as they talked about it. The dreadful disease of modern war which had started with artillery and cannon had escalated into the skinning and shrivelling of enemy bodies by atomic heat. And the nightmare did not end there. Who else would develop the bomb and use it, perhaps in the end sending the world up with it?

'The only thing,' said Helen now, with all the vehemence at her command, 'the only thing is it might be so terrible, war I mean, that people won't get into it in future. What do you think, Brendan?'

Moodily Brendan stuck a stalk of grass into his mouth.

'We're on our last chance, that's for sure.'

'We can pray,' said Rose. 'I think prayer is all that's left to us.'

'I don't believe in that,' said Helen. 'I think education's our best hope. Educating people out of their bigotry and hatred.'

'Putting decent boots on their feet, more like,' said Brendan. 'People don't go to war if they have decent homes, decent food, decent things to wear. I'm in politics because I believe in the reasonableness of the common man. Give him a fair deal and you'll get a fair deal back.'

'A lot of your union men aren't fair,' said Helen. Not all of her father's arguments had fallen on stony ground.

'And the bosses – *they're* a lovely lot, aren't they?' Brendan answered, not too seriously, because it was getting almost too hot. 'They're very good at listening and sharing, aren't they?'

Rose lay back and shut her eyes. 'Save your sarcasm,' she advised. 'We came out for a picnic. I just want a bit of hush and the sun on my face, for once.'

She lay thinking of Frankie Aarensen, who had sailed away after their wonderful six weeks together and who might have been at the battle called Iwo Jima that they had seen selected bits of on the cinema newsreels. She had not heard from him for months, but she just had this feeling about Iwo Jima and that maybe he had been there. Iwo Jima had got into her head and wouldn't be dislodged.

Frankie. She did not know what they did to kids in Chicago, but if Frankie was out of the mould, it was something good. Those clear eyes laughing into hers, his firm clasp on her waist when they danced. And how they'd danced. When she ran the film of their time together before her mind's eye they were always dancing and always laughing. She'd been important to Frankie in a way she'd never experienced before. He'd always put her first, opening doors for her, holding coats, listening to her as though what she said mattered. He'd made her over, really, into a new person. For that she would always be grateful. If that sounded as though she did not expect to see him again, then it was nothing but the truth. For she did not. Despite all his reassurances, his talk about the house with the orchard, the children, she was becoming more and more convinced that she would receive no more letters from Frankie Aarensen.

She would be no different from many other girls who had put their faith in the passing soldiery – or navy. You had to recognise that war did weird things to people's feelings. And although he had liked her, what did she amount to, really? Nothing much. Even the new grown-up person she saw herself as being. She was just a decent Catholic girl who hadn't shone at school, who had always been too conscious of her shabby clothes, her worn shoes, the hunger in the pit of her stomach, the need to look out for her younger brothers and sisters, to concentrate the way she should have done.

Maybe it would be just as well if she didn't hear from Frankie. Try as she might, she couldn't picture what it would be like in America, couldn't see how she could transform herself from an ordinary Glasgow typist into a wife who would have the care of a big house (as Frankie had promised) and who would have to get on with a whole network of hard-working, high-achieving relatives.

Frankie would find out in the end what she was really like. You had to be realistic and admit that the ability to dance up a storm together didn't exactly fit you for all the pitfalls of married life. She hadn't heard from him, anyhow. Maybe he had realised the minute he got away from her just how daft it had been to think he was in love with her.

She didn't confide any of this, even to Helen. Anyhow, unless at times like this, when she had a rare chance to sink into herself, decide what it was she felt and thought about things, she was just too busy. She had her job and with her mother sick, she had to keep the house running with the help of her out-of-work Dad and Brendan, to make sure Theresa, Ann-Marie, Kathleen, Hugh and Dermid went to school with their faces washed and hair combed, that they had something to eat at night, that they kept out of trouble. And when they remembered Bernadette and cried, she had to comfort them, even though she missed Bernadette more than any of them.

She turned to lie on her stomach and look at her brother and Helen. When she was with them, all three of them together like this, she always felt excluded. Odd man out. Funny that, since Helen was in love with Johnnie Dignam. But there was some kind of attraction, some kind of bond – between her brother and her best friend – it might just be that they were both what Rose thought of almost superstitiously, as 'scholars', people who had done well at school, who read and argued a lot and were 'bright'. She resented this difference even while she acknowledged it, for Brendan was her brother after all and the bond should be between *them*.

She turned full on her stomach and stared down at the grass. Would the affair between Helen and Johnnie Dignam come to any better end than the one between herself and Frankie? There had been that attempt to stop him seeing Helen, after all, and leopards weren't going to change their spots just because the war had ended. Johnnie was out in Berlin, trying to sort out the horrible mess the Germans found themselves in, using his gift for languages with the Germans and the Russians. He had been to the death camps. Rose sat up with a sudden resolution. She'd thought enough about things like atom bombs and death camps. She said a silent Hail Mary and gazed out at the sparkle of sunshine on the darkened water of the Clyde.

'I'm thinking,' said Helen, 'of going to London.' She looked at Brendan rather than Rose as she said this. 'I've been waiting to tell you.'

'You're out of your mind,' said Brendan swiftly. 'London? Now? Bomb craters everywhere, starving cats. Why would you go to London?'

'Because I've got a job.'

He didn't wait to hear what she had to say. Despite remonstrance from Rose, he jumped to his feet and looked heatedly down at Helen.

'So you're going to London just as the real job starts up here? To make something out of Glasgow. To make something out of Scotland. Great. It's as well to know who the traitors are, straight off.'

He shoved the heavy mass of dark hair off his forehead and looked so angry and put out, both girls laughed at his immoderation in spite of themselves. Nervous laughter.

'It's a free country,' Helen countered, with deceptive mildness.

'But it's what always happens. People fight a war then run out on what they were prepared to die for –'

'Brendan, hold your horses!' pleaded Rose. 'I'll miss Helen as much as you, but I'm not trying to stop her, am I?' She turned to her friend and said, 'What kind of job?'

'Secretary to a magazine called *Spectrum*.' She gazed at them defensively. 'It's only got a tiny circulation. But it's a foot in the journalistic door.'

'Run by some soft-centred Liberals,' said Brendan dismissively. 'I've heard of it. But I must be one of the few people who have.'

'Listen.' Helen tried to claim his serious attention. Her own stomach was churning in an alarming fashion because he was upset. 'When my sister Marie and the boys Rob and Alec are demobbed, what do you think it's going to be like at our place? It'll never hold us all. There'll be arguments all over the place between my dad and my brothers – sometimes in the old days it came to blows between them. I just want out. I want space to breathe and be my own woman. I want a career.' She rose up and her pale face, that had taken on a smattering of golden freckles from the summer sun, was more set and determined than Rose had ever seen it.

If only I could be like her, Rose thought. But I'll never be able to break away from the family. For who will look after the little ones in the ways that matter, cleaning their noses, drying their tears, if I'm not there? *That*, and missing Frankie Aarensen, as she would do till the end of her days.

Rose remained boneless on the travelling rug while Brendan followed Helen's slow, sauntering walk along the river bank. When he caught up with her, it took him all his time to stop crying out to her, 'Don't go! I want you to stay.' They weren't close enough for that. Whatever he might feel, they were really just platonic friends. But he tried to picture the landscape of his life without her and it would be like removing the sun, everything would go grey. He walked beside Helen, his head full of tumultuous emotions, his mouth turned down as mutinously as her own.

'There's nothing finalised between you and the army officer,' he said in desperation. He never called Johnnie by name, always referring to 'the army officer', imbuing it with all the contempt he could muster.

'What's that got to do with my taking a job in London?' She was taunting now, as angry as he was.

'Well, no doubt you'll want to be on hand, when he gets his demob. That's what it's all about, isn't it? You're going to take on his old dad and the rich girlfriend single-handed, aren't you?'

She gave him a look of pure fury and he knew he had hit his target.

'Johnnie's home is in the Cotswolds.'

'And London's a lot nearer the Cotswolds than Glasgow.'

'I'll see Johnnie, of course.' It was as much reassurance to herself as to him. Then she looked at him full-face, acknowledging all that he was saying to her, beneath the bluster; that he was trying to get her to face up to the possibility that she would never marry Johnnie. And in that moment Brendan Cassidy knew he loved Helen Maclaren because of her bravery and honesty.

He'd done his worst and all but destroyed the little citadel she clung to, that citadel of dreams that might turn out to be totally illusory. She was young and gauche, and argumentative and ambitious, and probably a bit silly and certainly romantic, but courage she was not short on. If Johnnie Dignam made life too painful for her, Brendan knew his own impulse would be to take him apart. Except that he was a pacific kind of man normally, a man who had been intended for the priesthood and who still carried a seed of conciliation within him that would not be extinguished. God, he understood nothing, nothing at the moment but his own pain.

What was this? Helen had taken his hand, looking back to make sure they were too far off for Rose to see the gesture. There were tears in her eyes as there were in his. His own skin burned to her touch, but he wanted more than the contact of hands. He wanted to pick her up, carry her off somewhere. He always wanted this when he saw her. To claim her.

'You'll need to look after Rose,' she was saying. 'She's got it into her head she'll never hear from Frankie again.'

'Maybe she won't. She hasn't had a letter from him for months.'

'She's had to carry a lot on her shoulders, with your mother being so sick.'

'Who will look after *me*?' he said, all the anger gone out of him at the touch of her hand. He could not bear it if she pulled it away.

She deflected his pain. 'Will you write to me?' she demanded. 'Will you write and tell me everything that's going on? Why should anything change about us being friends?'

'I don't know if I'll be any good at it.'

'You could come to London and see me. I could show you round.'

'You'll be the expert, will you?' But he was smiling at last.

'We could go to the House of Commons. So you'll know what to expect when you get to be an M.P. I'll be able to say to my journalist friends, "I knew him when he was just a shop steward." I think you'll get to be an M.P., Brendan, and that you'll do a lot for Glasgow. And I'll get to be a famous journalist, with my name on the side of a bus.'

'And pigs might fly.'

There was a letter awaiting her from Johnnie when she got home. She knew there would be something different about the contents for it looked just a normal, British-based letter, not like army mail that had been battered about and suffered the censor's pencil.

Her mother gave her a considering look as she hung the washing up on the brass chain across the chimney-piece. She hoped it would not be anything to upset her. Helen was volatile enough these days and Jessie wanted her daughter to go off to this new job in London in a more settled and happy frame of mind.

Helen gave her mother a half-apologetic look and took the letter into the front room to read. Ever since she and Johnnie had used the room it seemed redolent of his presence.

'Darling,' she read. 'You'll be astounded to know I am at home here on sick leave. I caught typhoid' – it might have been in the death camps, she thought with a stab of terror – 'and it seems convalescence is going to be a bit protracted. I have the energy of a flea and even writing tires me out.

'Peter Hart is dead. I can't write about it now. Wanted you to know what was going on and that I want to see you so very badly. But it will have to wait till I can cope – my father is fussing like a demented gnu. Take care, dearest girl. I'll write soon. Yours, Johnnie.'

She stood for a long while, just holding the letter. Why couldn't she go to him? She felt like a tree that had been flayed by the wind. *Tattery*. That was the word.

Tattery. Torn.

It was so good to hear from him, to feel the touch of him through the written word. But now the war was over she wanted more than that, she wanted the living, breathing person. He was back in Britain and he was sick and probably frightened and she couldn't go to him. He must be devastated by Peter's death – they were so close. She wondered briefly if her courage would extend to her turning up at Knoleberry Park and insisting that she should see him. A moment's reflection showed her the futility of the idea. She hadn't the money to go traipsing about in trains – it would take her all her time to save the fare to London for her new job. And although inside herself she knew her own worth, to go in and challenge the old English aristocracy about its attitudes made her knees tremble here, even now in her own home. Above all, Johnnie was pleading with her, between the lines, for her patience. He would undoubtedly get the best kind of care in his own home. She had waited this long and could entertain her worries about Johnnie's health a little longer. She put her hand up to her face and wiped away the tears. It wouldn't do to let her mother see she had been crying.

Five

When Helen went away to London, her mother Jessie missed her but upbraided herself for doing so. She worked relentlessly polishing the big steel grate in the tenement flat, changing curtains that did not need changing and cleaning windows that did not need cleaning. And when Kate Cassidy finally came home from the nuns' care, she was grateful for the chance to be a helpful neighbour. It took her mind off things and even Willie did not mind her helping 'that poor wee woman' now that Helen was far enough removed from Brendan. He was a prejudiced man often taken by surprise by his own sense of compassion.

'Your Rose looks as though somebody's stolen her scone these days,' said Jessie to Kate. 'Has she heard from her American sailor?'

'Never a word.' Kate poured herself a glass of stout. It was no use offering any to her temperance neighbour, but she felt the need of something to keep her going. She had no strength these days. No strength to lift so much as a darning needle or a dishcloth. She knew the children should have their hair cut and their underclothes changed more often, but she kept shoving the practicalities to the back of her mind. If she had enough to drink, she did not feel the darkest, deepest pain of all. That was her daily task. To find that level where nothing very much mattered, where she would not see Bernadette's big pleading eyes or see her stick-like under-nourished little body and where she would sometimes glimpse pleasure, happiness, like sunshine glinting through remembered trees.

'She's young enough,' Jessie offered. 'There'll be another man that's right for her. God knows, Kate, there's no hurry for any lass to tie herself to a man, when you think what's ahead of them, weans and trauchle* and work.'

As Kate nodded agreement, there was a loud knock at the door. 'Sit you where you are,' Jessie ordered and bustled down the lobby to see who the visitor was. Frankie Aarensen stood there in his United States Navy uniform, grinning from ear to ear, his eyes pleading for a welcome to match his expectations.

'Come in.' Jessie was temporarily speechless, but managed to add after a moment, 'I know someone who's going to be right surprised to see you.'

'When will she be in?' Frankie demanded of Rose's mother.

'Half past five she gets in,' said Kate, cautiously. 'Where have you been hiding yourself, Frankie, all this time?'

'She never thought to see you again,' Jessie chimed in. She said again, 'Will she be surprised to see you!' and then both women, remembering the strict rules of Glasgow hospitality, said together, 'Would you like a wee cup of tea?'

Rose had queued for bread during her lunch-hour and picked up some sausages for the tea. Like everybody else, she was fed up with having to queue for rationed bread now, when it hadn't been rationed all through the war. It was a dark, horrible colour and tasted terrible. It

* Stress.

seemed there was no end to doing without. Brendan said it was because America had suddenly stopped Lease-Lend, their wartime helping hand. Maybe they didn't like helping a Labour government.

She couldn't help thinking of Frankie and the whiff of luxury he'd brought into her life. It was almost like looking back at somebody else, remembering the carefree girl who had danced with him all those months ago.

Since he'd gone away, it was as if God had snatched away the colour in her life, leaving everything drab and defeated and changed. First Bernadette, whose gentle, stoic suffering and death burned like a white candle in the mind. Then her mother's illness. What could be done about the drinking that both her parents now indulged in, as though caught up in some mutual compulsion not to think, not to be rational? Was it because they both felt like challenging the priest, and God – as she did – but did not have the courage? And despite her best efforts, the younger children were growing wild and ungovernable. At times, despite Brendan's support and help, she felt as though she were drowning and helpless in her sea of troubles. And worst of all, there was this great stony certainty that she would never extricate herself from her situation, would never be strong and enterprising and sure of herself, like Helen. Now that Frankie had forsaken her, she would stay here and wipe noses and restrain fighting children till the end of time. Even if he ever came back, she would have to do the same. Somehow this definition of being good remained in her mind as though by doing all the unlovely necessary tasks she somehow held the Cassidy identity together. But she wavered. How she wavered! How she wanted to spend some of the money she earned on herself!

She turned into the close and registered the fact that

the flat door was open. Her youngest sister, Theresa, dashed through it, shouting, 'Here she is!' and then dashed back in again. She could hear more raised voices and Sam barking, and laughter, and her heart raced so hard she thought it would leap out of her throat.

'He's here! Frankie's here. Look!' Theresa shouted and Rose had only time to think the child might have washed her grubby face before he was standing in front of her, snub nose, piercing blue eyes just exactly as before (exactly) and her arms were rising without her sanction to meet his outstretched ones and her mouth was surrendering itself to his firm one. Abashed, after a moment she stood back, aware of her drab coat, her hair tangled by the wind and rain and the joshing satisfaction of her siblings' chorus. Even Jessie smiled though on the periphery of her vision Rose knew her mother did not: her mother sat as still as a statue of the Madonna with her lips close together and her dark eyes burning with that dull anxiety that never left them. Even if a moment later she too smiled, Rose did not forget that look.

'You never wrote.' The words were torn from her, as though they had been battering to get out as indeed they had been all these months. 'I wrote to you.'

'And I to you.' How could she not believe it, when he had his arms around her? 'I wrote but they must have gone down, all the letters, in the Pacific. I was a prisoner after that – after the ship caught it – and I was picked up by the Japs. Never mind all that. I'll tell you everything later. I'm here now. That's what matters. Here now to see about getting you back to America with me. Tell me you're pleased to see me, Rose!'

His ship had put into the Clyde for repairs and he was determined to use the brief time at his disposal to persuade Rose to become one of the 50,000 G.I. brides and fiancées being 'processed' for life in the States in a camp in southern England.

At first she did not hear him. Her mind refused to register the words. 'You're here,' she said. 'Actually here. After all. I can't believe it.' All she wanted to do was to touch him to reassure herself he was safe, to be with him to hear what he'd been through. It was enough to be going out with him again, to the pictures to see *Brief Encounter*, to the dance halls to waltz or jitterbug or foxtrot, reviving the magic of the first time they'd been together.

Jessie Maclaren, observing from the sidelines, thought soberly it was as though the girl sprang to life again. Colour had come back into her cheeks, she had found the money somehow (probably from Brendan) for a new pair of shoes and a tie-neck blouse. She clung to Frankie as though to life itself, whether it was at the windy stop waiting for a tram or going in the close mouth with fish suppers for the family.

Rose did not stop this time to wonder how far she should let him go. There was a weakness, a lack of resistance in her that frightened her, a dependence on him as though for the breath in her body. He said he loved her and she wanted to be made over by his love, made new and different and strong. She wanted him claiming her body and altering her from under-privileged family skivvy to strong, loved, independent woman. It was the only way she would be able to strike away the bonds of family and she had no option but to grasp it.

'We'll get married in Chicago,' he said. 'It will be a sign of our new life. We'll get married where we're going to settle down. You can buy all the clothes you need when you come out there.'

She let herself be carried forward by the tide, let him start the formalities that would take her out to him as his bride. The night before he rejoined his renovated ship, they took a tram to Queen's Park and there in the chilly dark they made love with a kind of slow and formal reverence, shutting out everything except their need for each other.

'I want you, Rose,' he said with utter certainty. She brushed grass from her skirt and they returned to the centre of the city, the night not over yet, and danced in the Playhouse to 'Smoke Gets in Your Eyes'. She had no regrets. She was growing into a new person, a woman who would have a home of her own, with a man who wanted to work and provide for her. It occurred to her she would have a lot of dignity and once you had dignity it was like roots. It would make everything possible.

Wouldn't it?

'I don't know,' Jessie Maclaren wrote to her daughter in London in her neat, precise hand, 'what is going to happen across the landing. Things seem to go from bad to worse. When Joe Cassidy goes out drinking now, Kate goes with him. The bairns have to fend for themselves, unless Rose is around and she doesn't get home from work till six. And *she* looks as white as a clout now Frankie's gone.

'Brendan goes about as though he has all the cares of the world on top of him. I think he wears the same collar from one week's end to another. But that's enough of other folk's troubles. I hope you're not working too hard and are getting enough to eat.'

Helen tucked the letter away thoughtfully in her handbag. It was some time since she'd heard from Brendan. When he did write, it was all fairly high-minded stuff about philosophy or politics, half-digested, she felt, out of books and probably intended to impress her. She would write him a cheery note, telling him about some of the dusty and eccentric politics she'd met through her job on the magazine.

She stared through the dusty attic windows of the

Bloomsbury premises of *Spectrum*, suddenly and sharply
nostalgic for her home, for her mother's voice, even for
the rain and wind that battered you in that improvident
place, Glasgow. It wasn't that she didn't like London.
You couldn't help but sense the stoic nobility of the
place, the way it had come through the war, and the
grass and London Pride growing all over the bomb
sights brought out a kind of tender, nursing response in
her. But it was vast, so many streets, so many people. It
brought home to you in a quite devastating way at times
a sense of your own insignificance. Glasgow folk were
strangers to this feeling. Heavens! She put a hand up to
the corner of her eye and felt it wet. Fancy getting
nostalgic for wind and rain and rackety old trams, even
that damp old close mouth with its smelly white tiles.
She mustn't be a softie.

Hugh Latimer, the big, shambling Highland Scot who
was her editor, came out of his rabbit-hutch of an office
and raised a bushy eyebrow at her. (Both eyebrows were
like flue-brushes and a dark, glistening red, like his
shoulder-length hair).

'Got nothing to do, Helena?' He often used this
theatrical version of her name, amusing her, as did
nearly everything about this big, gentle, erudite man,
with his shabby suede shoes, deplorable tweed jacket
and musical voice that had a disconcerting habit of
breaking on the occasional high note. Hugh Latimer
was nobody's fool, however. Through the open door of
his rabbit-hutch he'd heard the distinct sound of a
breath drawn in like a sob.

Helen shook her head. 'I've finished the typing.'

'Write me something then.'

She looked at him astounded. Once or twice he had
given her theatre tickets and asked for a brief review.
Once he'd let her review a novel. But the few pieces
she'd written of her own volition lay unused on his desk.

They'd been short impressionistic essays about being a newcomer to London, about feeding the stray cats in Gray's Inn Road, intended for tucking away at the end of the magazine after all the heavy polemical stuff.

'I mean it. I need five hundred words for page twelve. On what you got out of a Scottish education.'

Again she stared at him, about to protest she couldn't do it. Not just like that. Off the top of her head.

'Listen, Helena,' he said, good-naturedly. He put his head down close to her face. 'The compleat journalist should be able to look out that window over there and give you five hundred words on the first object you see. And another thing. Never say "no can do". Always say "can do". That way, my dear girl, you'll rise to the top like cream in Gaelic coffee.'

She began to smile despite her wistfulness.

'Righto, Mr Latimer,' she said. 'Can do.'

'Make it Hugh. That's another thing to remember. The journalist doesn't kowtow. The journalist needs hubris. Bloody cheek. The journalist is the Fourth Estate. Remember that, young Helena. The journalist is the people. One of these days you'll have to get out of this dug-out. There's no money and not much scope. But I'll teach you what I can and you can go forth and do better.'

It was the longest speech Hugh Latimer had ever made. After it, he put on the deplorable felt hat that went with the deplorable tweed jacket and a deplorable once-white raincoat and disappeared. Helen sat alone in the office and faced a blank sheet of paper.

'My English teacher,' she began to type, 'once threw a volume of Ibsen on to my desk and said, "See what you make of that." No explanation of who Ibsen was. I didn't know him from butter. She knew I had a desperation inside me to find out. She said, "I can't tell you the truths of literature. I can only point the way." Was she a lazy teacher or a good one?'

She was off now. Her typing had become so good that her fingers now kept up with her brain. She made mistakes, but she simply crossed them out and got on with it. Writing had never been difficult for her. Unconsciously since coming to work for Latimer, she had picked up good habits of conciseness, of being plain but vivid. 'Paper's scarce,' he would growl remindingly. 'Bare bones, lassie. Bare bones.'

She loved the challenge of words. Of getting down what she thought and felt then trimming it, polishing it, till it shone like a jewel in its own right. She worked over the task Latimer had set her till she was almost satisfied then put her cover on her machine. She was beginning to feel hungry. She thought she might walk up Shaftesbury Avenue and have something to eat in the Lyons Corner House at Piccadilly.

When she let herself out of the office and locked up, Johnnie Dignam was waiting for her just a few steps away. It was always a shock to see him in civilian clothes, in the good, shabby prewar tweeds he wore, instead of army uniform. She had loved him in uniform. It might have been made for such as Johnnie. That was not to say she didn't love him in tweeds. However he was dressed, he turned her blood to water in that first moment she saw him after any separation. She had not expected to see him tonight. They kissed and he took her arm possessively. 'Where are we going?' he demanded. He fell in with her suggestion of the Corner House. 'You look lovely,' he said in her ear. 'I've been wanting to see you all day, wondering if you're really as lovely as I think. And you are.' They stopped and kissed again and a middle-aged woman, skirting round them, hissed with annoyance then smiled in spite of herself.

'Darling,' she said, when they had chosen their food and were seated at a corner table, 'are you supposed to be up in London again?' She touched his thin cheek anxiously. 'Are you better? Stronger?'

He caught her hand. 'I've been up seeing a new man, a specialist, a psychiatrist. The latest thinking is that the insomnia and stomach pains I'm getting now have nothing to do with the original typhoid, that it's an anxiety neurosis, arising out of what I saw.'

'What you saw in the camps?'

'This chap I saw today, he sees plenty of servicemen, it seems. Blokes who've been on the Murmansk run or other convoys, pilots who've been shot down – and those who went into Auschwitz and Belsen and the other places.'

'War trauma.'

'I remember you saying you'd read up on psychology. This chap I saw seems a good enough egg. Seems I'll have to talk a lot of it out, even go back to childhood to find out what made me the kind of bloke I am.'

'Do you really think it'll help? I know what kind of bloke you are. Kind and nice and sensitive. I wish I'd known you were coming. That you'd given me a ring. I would like to have looked forward to seeing you. I would have worn something nicer.'

'I'd meant to catch an earlier train back. I'm supposed to be home for my stomach medication. But I couldn't come to London and not see you. That's what I decided. *You're* my best medicine.'

She looked at him tremulously. They had seen each other three times since she had come to London and still there was no invitation forthcoming to his home in the Cotswolds.

The first time she had seen him she had been shocked to her very core. He had looked so papery and thin, as though the first wind that came along would blow him away. Only his blue eyes had burned like two flags of defiance and then the smile, that devastating smile, had been the same. She had held him, that first time, as though he were a child, afraid to express too much joy in case it would crush him.

If there were ends to tie up, still, with Simonette, things to be sorted out between Johnnie and his father, she could not rush matters. Johnnie's convalescence and restoration to full health were all that mattered. She wrote to him three times a week. His letters were less frequent, but longer. She treasured them because she felt the true man was revealed in them, funny, percipient, full of insights. Maybe she was not as shocked as she might have been about his seeing the psychiatrist because she knew deep down there was a spirit that could not be quenched. He had simply been asked for a time to bear burdens, physical and spiritual, that would have been too much for any man.

She could not help it. If he was suffering, she wanted to be his comfort. The tomato soup that she had thought she wanted congealed on its dish, unwanted, and she wept.

'Don't,' he begged urgently. He passed a clean handkerchief from his lap to hers. As she blew into it he said fiercely, 'I miss you too. Don't you believe that?'

Six

The Corner House's 'orchestra' that evening consisted of two sad-looking, elderly Poles and a lady cellist of indeterminate shape wearing a headband in the 'twenties manner. The music they made had a haunting, wailing quality underneath the surface sprightliness. Johnnie surveyed them moodily while Helen cast her eye round their fellow-diners. Despite the women's jaunty hats and bright slashes of lipstick, the general impression was of the threadbare, of a desperate effort to keep things going. People had had the energy sucked out of them by the war and instead of being rewarded now they were being asked to tighten their belts and then tighten them yet again. Helen wondered idly what it had been like in Piccadilly before the war, when the gilded rich had driven up to the Café de Paris in their leather-redolent saloons, the women draped in animal furs, the men in penguin suits. She'd read somewhere that the period before the first war had been like one long golden afternoon, never recaptured. Was paradise receding further and further from the human race, punishment for each of their wars?

Johnnie's voice broke into her reverie.

'Can I stay with you tonight?'

She felt the colour recede from her face. 'Won't they be waiting for you – back home?'

'I'll ring and tell them I'm staying at the Empire Club.'

Their eyes met and they looked away. She was perfectly aware what he was suggesting. In her sparsely furnished room at Lancaster Gate, at the top of a stuccoed, once-pretty house that overlooked Hyde Park, she had often imagined him sitting opposite her at the patchily-varnished table with its barley-sugar legs.

She had conducted conversations with him in her head while she toasted cheese for her supper in the marginal kitchen, in the ancient bath with its five inches of water, and in the creaky sofa-bed with its mingy blankets she had imagined lying in his arms and knowing the contact of skin on skin.

But she was her mother's daughter and every admonition, every shibboleth, came back to warn her now. Nice girls didn't. Nice girls waited. But it was a question of what must now be uppermost in her life and that was being with Johnnie. Her mother was in Glasgow, after all. The legions of the Wee Free were receding into the mists of Gaeldom. In some curious way she was as committed to Johnnie as she was to her own life. She could not keep the two existences from intermingling and what she felt was suddenly many times as powerful as conventional bonds.

'All right. I make my own moral decisions.' There. It was out. And she felt a soaring sense of freedom almost straight away. 'We'll have to be careful how I take you in. I don't want the landlady to know.' The landlady, to whom she'd been recommended by a friend of Hugh Latimer, was a stout, maternal North Italian, claiming bonds 'because we both come from the mountains'. (That Glasgow wasn't exactly mountain country was something Helen had kept from her, not wanting to deny the sentiment in her first homesick days.)

She felt his hand claim hers, rub the signet ring he had bought her. 'My dearest girl,' he said. 'I love you with all my soul.'

'I won't,' he said feverishly. 'I won't be separated from you.'

They made love all the night through and she was struggling up through the chains of passion to the realisation that it would soon be time to go and work for Hugh Latimer. How she would be able to bring herself down to the ordinary everyday plane she still didn't know. Her head was in Elysium. His wiry body had been unbelievably wonderful and strange to her. Echoing in her mind were his own words of love and wonder as he discovered her. But she wanted it all again. She wanted the experience repeated till it was imprinted in every gene and every corpuscle. If you imagined endless dancing, when your limbs were as light as air and the music came from some heavenly source, that was what it was like, being together. She had known it, from the moment his hand had gone round her waist at that staid 'Servicemen's Soirée' in the church hall. Even then, it had been like stepping off the edge of the world. She stopped trying to encompass how she felt with mere words and similes. It was unlike anything she had ever known. It was like being re-clothed in a different skin, reborn in a different world ... There, she was at it again.

'Why are you smiling?' he said tenderly.

She said nothing.

'Did I make you happy?'

She put her arms up and pulled his mouth on to hers. After this she would get up and wash and put on her pale blue jumper and her navy suit and go out into that strange new place, the world. How wonderful it would be! She suddenly wanted to recompense all the dull places, the dark places, the wounded places, for the happiness she had been given. She had not known that love could make you invincible.

'Oho,' said Hugh Latimer, with an amused look, 'so

"the lark's in the bush," is he; "the snail's on the thorn." Who is this guy, who's put all right with your world, madam?'

Helen put the pile of letters to be signed in front of her boss.

'He's an army officer,' she confessed. 'He caught typhoid in Belsen and nearly died. Now he's getting better.'

'What's his name?' quizzed Latimer.

'Dignam, Captain Johnnie Dignam, M.C.'

'The young hero of Sicily?' Latimer, despite his carefully nurtured persona of the woolly intellectual, of county squire turned champion of the people, had a sharp journalistic recall. 'Is he a Gloucester Dignam? His father that old Hitler appeaser, Sir Bertram Dignam?'

'His father's Sir Bertram. He was a war hero, too. Of the First War. He lost a leg. Johnnie is very close to his father.'

'Well, the boy may have cleaned some of the muck off the family escutcheon, but Dignam *père* went to Berchtesgarden and fratted with Hitler, Ribbentrop and the rest of the ghastly crew.'

She could feel the hair stand up on the back of her neck and then perspiration run down the middle of her spine.

'Even Chamberlain had to buy time for us. We weren't ready for a war.'

'I don't think Dignam was just an appeaser. I think he went along with the thinking of the jolly old Fascisto. When the war broke out, he about-faced, of course, but there are those of us with long memories. Who don't trust some of the *ancien régime*. Still, I do not impugn your lover-boy. He had a good war. What do the aristos down at Knoleberry Park think of a wee working-class lassie from the Gorbals?'

'I'm not from the Gorbals.' She saw he was teasing and let her voice drop from its dramatic note. 'I don't know. I haven't met them yet.'

'Oh, keep away, hen,' said Latimer. 'You're too nice for the likes of them. Stick to a career. Marriage is strictly for the birds, anyhow.'

'I thought you were a democrat,' she said, evenly. Arguing with Hugh Latimer never fazed her. She was too used to the hurly-burly of Glaswegian polemics.

Latimer was clearly intrigued by the romance his secretary was having with a scion, as he called it, of one of the oldest families in England. Helen knew she was too young and green for him to be interested in her in any personal sense – she thought if anything he was congenitally anti-women anyhow – but in a way a genuine relationship was building up between them, one of a joshing kind of trust.

He was amazed by the insouciance of an eighteen-year-old who sometimes even wore ankle sox but who could argue as hard as any Clydeside navvy. He was tickled by her practical aptitude for running the office, dealing with late contributors, coping with extra work without getting flustered. He had lived with a number of soft and indulgent old aunts who'd never had to cope with anything more demanding than a wheezy Pekinese and this brisk, bright, doughty young female with her bouncing red-gold hair was a new phenomenon. If men didn't look out, women like these would be running the postwar world. He liked the girl, though, and surprised himself by feeling quite proprietorial. Feeling avuncular was new to him, but he was prepared to bring her on, give her a chance. On days when the office was quiet he took her out for a pub lunch, introducing her judiciously to some Fleet Street names and at other times doing his best to fill in the considerable gaps in her education and manners, to guide her reading and thinking.

Learning that she liked poetry, he took her to some pub poetry readings and once pointed out Dylan Thomas to her.

'Your lover-boy will follow father into the Tory party, no doubt,' he said, one day when they were seated in the Mucky Duck (or Black Swan) eating cheese and bread and desultorily watching people shake hats and umbrellas as they came in out of the rain.

'But the party will change,' she said, vehemently. 'Johnnie has told me. The war did to him what the first one did to Harold Macmillan – made him think of his men, what they were coming back to. The Tories will institute a lot of reforms and Johnnie says they can generate wealth for the country in a way Labour cannot.'

'H'mm,' said Latimer, gazing abstractedly into his beer, 'maybe it's taken another bloody war to make pragmatism popular. It'll be something if the day of the ranting demagogue is no more. "The best lack all conviction, while the worst are full of passionate intensity'."

'You're quoting Yeats,' she said sharply, 'but didn't he and a lot of other poets and so-called thinkers flirt with Fascism?' She gazed directly into Latimer's face. 'Was Johnnie's father the only one?'

'He did it more publicly than most.' Latimer drained his glass unrepentantly. 'C'mon. We've got work to do. The centre's got to hold this time round, girl. That's where the likes of you and me have to direct our energies.'

She looked at his filthy pipe, clamped like a baby's comforter between his teeth.

'You know what the doctors are saying in Buffalo?'

'No, I don't. What are the doctors saying in Buffalo?'

'That one day, years from now, they'll prove smoking is bad for you. That it causes cancer.'

'C'mon, Cassandra. You're my secretary, not my mammy.'

Are you never going to ask me down to Knoleberry?

Although it was enough just to be with Johnnie, to walk through the park with him, sit in the news cinema watching Winston Churchill talk about the Iron Curtain coming down on Europe, share a Chelsea bun with him in a coffee bar, take him to her room, and make love with him, the unsatisfactoriness of not meeting his family – he had met hers, after all – was poisoning everything they did.

Obviously he did not want to talk about it. In the beginning, she had gone along with that, because of the state of his health and because it had been enough just to be with him. But now she knew the obstacles had not gone away. Somewhere in the background his father was exerting influence that would mean Johnnie marrying one of his own kind, with money to bolster the estate. She knew there was talk of getting Johnnie to stand for Parliament at the next election, even though he still talked hopefully about earning a living from writing. But while it had not seemed fair to hassle him while his health was threatened, now he was beginning to look and feel better surely her feelings merited some consideration?

A tension was building up between them that she did not know how to deal with and he would not help by giving her an opening. When they met, it was after sessions with his therapist and he sometimes wore a flayed and desperate look. When he told her anything, it was allusive and incomplete. But if he did not talk to her soon, about the matters that most closely affected him, they were going to drift apart at some deep and elemental level, the level where they had first met. Physical reassurance, the touch and the kiss, much though they both wanted them and needed them, were not going to be enough.

He dragged her off one evening to a huge orchestral concert at the Albert Hall, Mahler and Beethoven. She knew little about classical music and the enormous battery of sound came crashing down on her senses like a mountain avalanche.

Afterwards, going back to her place through Hyde Park, it was clear the music had had a profound effect on him. Jealously she listened while he hummed passages that were familiar to him, unable to respond in a similar manner.

'I'm only just starting out,' she acknowledged. 'I'll understand it one day.'

He looked at her aggrieved, determined face and then responded with that sensitivity she had never had from anyone else. He put his arms around her and kissed her briefly on the lips. 'You will have to suffer a little first,' he suggested.

'Why?'

'Do you think I want it to be so? I want you to live in perpetual sunlight, my darling. But you are human and suffering is part of the human condition.'

'I've known hardship,' she claimed.

'Not the same.'

'And sorrow.' She thought of the child who had died across the landing, the little sister of Rose and Brendan.

He was quiet. They walked on with their arms around each other. 'I think, whatever happens,' he said, 'that you will have a good life, Helen. How exciting for you, to be just beginning the journey. So young, so sure, so strong.'

She shook him gently. 'You talk like Methuselah.'

'I've been a long way.' It was one of his allusive remarks and she knew it referred to the camps, to what he had seen in Europe.

'I wish you could tell me a little.'

'I can't.'

'If you could only share it –'

When they were in bed they were very tender with each other. When they were separated, afterwards, lying back-to-back in post-coital attitudes, she suddenly heard him give a great sigh that was more of a moan. He began to punch his pillow.

'They had an orchestra, you know, made up of the inmates, the musicians, the wonderful violinists and cellists and the rest, and they had to play for the men who did these dreadful things, who made parchment for lamps out of human skin and soap from the oils of the human body.'

He began to weep with a lack of restraint that frightened her.

'The first day I went in there, Helen, there was this human being coming towards me and she was no more than a skeleton, a bone wrapped in a rag. Her eyes were open but what was there wasn't alive. She held out a hand to me and then she sank to her knees and keeled over and just died. I can't forget that look – it said "Too late, too late".

'There is just so much rage in me I don't know where to put it. I don't know how to live with it, any more than she did.'

'It will pass.' She didn't know where the words came from, though they were hers. She felt her mouth parched beyond bearing.

'That is what Dr Bering says.'

'Then if he can say it, you can believe it.'

And what about your father? She asked the question in her mind. Had he made it easier for the Nazis and did it make it harder for Johnnie now?

Seven

'What's the matter, Mammy? Are you not feeling well?'

Rose Cassidy had just come home from work to find the gas mantle turned down low in the kitchen, none of the children at home and the table not set, even in her mother's hasty slapdash manner, for tea. Her mother had climbed into one of the set-in beds and was barely visible above the quilt and blankets. The fire was almost smothered in ash and clinkers. Rose caught the smell of crisis.

Kate Cassidy opened her eyes as though by a mighty effort. 'It's your Da, Rose,' she said. 'They've taken him in for being drunk and disorderly and for hitting a polisman. He didn't know what he was doing, Rose, he never meant for to hurt anybody, you know your Da.' Kate sat up in a rough tousled heap and the hot, sweet fumes of whisky mac floated in the direction of her daughter.

Rose barely wasted a glance on her parent. 'Where are the kids?' she demanded. 'What's happened to them?'

'They've been taken in, by the Corporation. Brendan tried to get it stopped, but they wouldna' listen to him –'

'When did this happen?'

'A wee while ago.'

'Where's Brendan now?'

'Trying to raise bail for tomorrow morning, for your Da.'

Rose sat down suddenly, as though her legs would no longer hold her up.

'Ma, I've seen it coming. Maybe this'll put a stop to it now, the drinking.'

'It's to give me the strength,' said Kate, confusedly. 'I'm that weak, Rose, sure there's no strength in my bones. I want my bairns back –' Her voice rose in an anguished wail. 'They cannae take my bairns away from me, they've nae right to do that, Rose. You go down the City Chambers for me, tell them I've been in poor health but I'm getting out of it, Rose, I'm getting better.'

'Oh, Mother.' Rose could not hide the worn impatience. 'You'll never be any different now, you and Da. You promised Brendan. He's at the end of his tether and so am I. I'm having a bairn now too, Mammy. I was sick at the office today and they know and I'm not going back. I can't face it.'

Kate rose up in the huddled bed and put unsteady white legs over the side. The beds were set high in the wall and you needed the aid of a chair to step out of them. She drew on her skirt and darned jumper, doing her best to fight off the effects of the drink she had taken earlier in the day.

'I don't believe it. I never heard you say it, did I? My poor lassie. No' you, Rosie? I thought you knew better. O gentle Mary, Mother of God! No' another mouth to feed ...'

Kate's actions belied her words. She tried to raise up her daughter's face and to kiss it. She wiped the hair tenderly back from Rose's forehead, staring into the defeated, expressionless eyes. 'But we'll manage, Rose. We've always managed somehow,' she babbled. 'The Lord will provide.'

'I don't want it,' said Rose with certainty. 'I never want

a child.'

'Don't,' pleaded Kate. 'Sure there's worse than a babby.' But she was staggering about the dimly-lit kitchen, directionless and incapable. 'Make us a cup o' tea, Rose,' she pleaded. 'I'll be right in a minute.'

The Procurator-Fiscal wanted to be finished with the morning's proceedings, which had been repetitive and wearying to a degree. Gang warfare, prostitutes turning a trick, drunks and disorderlies. He turned a harsh judicial gaze on Bailie Drummond set at an intimidating angle above him.

'The accused and his wife are in the habit of visiting drinking dens, your Honour, and imbibing as much as they can before closing time. They have been given warnings but have shown truculence which, I am sorry to say, on this occasion turned to more than that; turned into a veritable *fracas* in which a police constable was injured and members of the public set at risk.'

The reporters on the press bench wrote 'fracas' in their notebooks and smirked at one another, enjoying the Procurator's predictable long-windedness.

'Thirty days without the option,' said Bailie Drummond who was also fed up with the length of the proceedings. To Joe Cassidy, whose head was sunk deep into his chest, he said upbraidingly 'And I don't want to see you here again. Take him down, constable.'

Outside the court, Kate looked beseechingly at Brendan. Today she was quite a smart little woman, presentable in a borrowed navy coat with her hair neatly combed. Brendan shrugged. 'That's it,' he said heavily. 'You heard what the man said.'

Back at the house the table was neatly laid out with cups and saucers and a plate of biscuits. Rose had combed Theresa's dark curls and tied them up with a blue ribbon and then done Anne-Marie's hair and

Kathleen's in plaits. Even the boys, Hugh and Dermid, looked preternaturally tidy and clean. For once, although they fidgeted and sometimes poked one another, the children were quiet. They had been threatened with going back to the home if they didn't behave.

Two people sat on the hard chairs in front of the set-in beds. Shona Macbride, Kate Cassidy's younger sister, and her solicitor husband, Kevin, had come all the way from Dublin at the behest of the children's grandmother, but had not been able to drag themselves to the disgrace of the court. They had the customary pink composure of the petit bourgeoisie. By contrast to the Cassidy family they looked well, even expensively, dressed, and certainly better fed.

'You understand, Kate,' said Shona now, 'it's Mother's wish that we should have the children for a while. They'll get country air on the farm and Kevin won't take any nonsense from them.' She turned to her husband, 'Will you, Kevin?' He gave the two boys, who were indulging in a little light wrestling, a reproving glare, before assuring his wife, manfully, 'Certainly not.'

'You'll not be too hard on them?' demanded Kate. 'They'll be good children. They have goodness in them.' She turned to the children and said, 'Sure, I'll be right soon and you'll all come back. Be good to your grannie and your Aunt Shona and Uncle Kevin.'

'It's for the best,' said Shona, unnerved by her sister's terrible composure. 'Sure we couldn't see them going into homes.'

'Can we ride the donkeys, Auntie Shona?' demanded Kathleen.

'Can we milk the cows?' asked Theresa.

'Will we go on the big boat?' This was Anne-Marie, on a tremulous note.

'I'll make the tea,' said Rose tonelessly.

Shona looked at her eldest niece. 'Don't forget,' she

chivvied, 'to get yourself down to the doctor's for a tonic, Rose.' No one had enlightened her about the baby, but maybe she had her suspicions because she said in a gentle tone, 'And once we've had the tea, we'd best get moving.'

The children began to cluster round her instead of their mother and she, the childless one, was suddenly in charge of ribbons that wouldn't stay tied and shoe-laces that needed doing-up, noses that needed wiping. The faces of her husband and sister were open maps, the one of chivvied doubt, the other of helpless despair.

'Brendan,' said Rose Cassidy quietly. 'Can you lend me the money for the bus to London? I think it's thirty bob – less than the train.'

Brendan looked up from his book. Since the family calamities he had withdrawn into himself and seldom addressed either Rose or his parents. When Kate and the recently-released Joe had tidied themselves up earlier to go out for what was to be a night's drinking, though they both vehemently denied it, saying they were going visiting, he had simply said nothing. He had stopped going to night school and even attending his political meetings, wanting merely to read and sleep and submit to the ennui that served as a kind of baffle wall between him and his feelings.

'What are you talking like that for?' he demanded, with a guilty irritability. 'Have you written to him out there yet, the chap from the Windy City? Does he know about the baby?'

She shook her head. 'He's not going to know. I'm not going out to him.'

Patiently he quizzed: 'Why not? I thought all the arrangements were to hand.'

'I can't face it. Going out there with my stomach

sticking out. They're pan loaf,* his family. I was to be married in white. I'm not going out to have them pointing the finger at me –'

'It's his, as well as yours.'

'I can get it adopted. In London.'

'You're not being rational. For God's sake, Rose, use a bit of common sense –'

'I'll be what I like!' She was shouting at him, white-faced and in danger of losing control. 'It's me it's happening to, it's me that'll decide. I want to get away from this house, this family, I don't care where I go. I'm not going to be like *her*' – she gesticulated towards her mother's empty chair – 'one baby after another till she's turned to mush. I don't care what anybody says, I don't want it, I don't want it.'

He got up reluctantly from his chair and put his arms around her, making soothing noises. 'Where would you go in London?' He tried to get her to see reason.

'To Helen Maclaren's. She'd put me up.'

'She's got one room.'

'She's my friend.'

'You can't take our troubles into her life. We've got to sort them out for ourselves. Would you like me to write to Frankie? It's him you should be turning to –'

'I hate him!' she cried wildly.

'I thought you loved him.'

'After this!' She crashed her fists down on her stomach. 'It hasn't happened to him, has it? The men get off scot-free.'

'You're talking a lot of wild, daft nonsense.' He said it with unwonted gentleness. Her mention of Helen Maclaren had set something alive in his own mind, so that he suddenly wanted to see Helen again, talk to her. Rose wasn't the only one who missed her and wanted to

* Respectable.

be where she was. She hadn't married the Englishman yet. In fact, in her last letter she hadn't even mentioned him. It was all about the writing she was doing, the people she was meeting through Hugh Latimer. He was filled with an aching, desperate need to follow her, to breathe the same air, share the same excitements. He, who had talked relentlessly against leaving Glasgow, forsaking Scotland, did not want to live there any more because of what had happened. Wanted to escape, get away from the crushing bonds of family, hold his head up, be a new and different man. Worst of all to bear was people's pity. One colleague had put it into words: 'I'm sorry about your family, Brendan. You're a decent enough man yourself. You keep off the drink and all that.' He'd wanted to scream at the man, justify his parents, but he couldn't do that, he was known as a quiet and rational man. But they would put him down. They would all be tarred with the same dissolute brush. They wouldn't give him respect and they wouldn't vote for him. They were hard bloody judges. The same wild, passionate need that Rose was voicing for autonomy, for finding oneself, was sounding like a tocsin in his own head. But he was mixed up, too, maybe even more than she was. There was no basis in reality for the fantasies of seeing Helen Maclaren again. She'd made all that clear a long time ago.

Rose stalked the room, her pale, tear-stained face lit up by a furious, accusatory glare.

'If you don't give the money, I'll pawn something.'

He spread his hands. 'I haven't got it, Rose.'

She went over to the kitchen window, turning the cold water tap on and off, finally pushing her head under the spurt of liquid and taking a noisy gulp. Then she turned a hard, stranger's face to her brother and said, 'Tell them nothing about this. You hear?'

She couldn't go. He made allowances for her

hysterical reaction. Eventually she would calm down and in the meantime whether she liked it or not, he would write to Frankie Aarensen and apprise him of the true state of affairs. He put his faith in Frankie. He should have been more careful, not got the poor girl in the family way, but Brendan had always felt Frankie was a decent bloke, not just out for what he could get.

'I'll not say a word,' he calmed her. Having got some of the fear and rage out of her system, she would put the mad notion of London out of her mind. It was too heart-breaking to think of her getting on that bus with wild intentions of having the baby adopted. He made up his mind to break his own inertia and keep an eye on her. She was, after all, missing their younger brothers and sisters who, from all accounts, were taking to the farm if not necessarily school with its firm, convent-based authority.

He fell asleep worrying how he could help Rose to think more clearly about her dilemma. He would take her out to the pictures the following evening, to cheer her up, and maybe buy her tea at Cranston's Tearooms first.

But when he got home the following evening from work, she was gone and the house was in uproar, with Jessie Maclaren shunting in and out with Askit headache powders for his mother, Kate alternately weeping and shouting threats of what she would do when she got Rose back, Joe sitting silent, stunned and guilty and various relatives picking up the note Rose had left on the table, reading it incredulously then throwing it back down among the crumbs and empty porter bottles.

'The traitress!' cried Kate. 'To pawn my linen sheets, my treasures, that the good little sisters back in Clare sewed for me, with the drawn-thread work and all. Never, even when I hadn't a lump of coal for the fire or

a crust to put in my children's mouths, have I not
retrieved them from the pawnshop when I could. Oh,
she'll roast in hell for this!' She gazed at Sam, Frankie's
dog. 'And she says look after you. Where's him that
saved you?' Sam gazed back at her, desperately trying to
sort out the message behind the timbre of her voice.
Conciliatory, he went and sat on his blanket.

The traitress of the sheets sat meanwhile in the
ramshackle bus taking its usual quota of straitened Scots
to the capital. A sticky infant in a satin bonnet puked,
whimpered and slept in her mother's arms next to her,
while in the seat in front a drunk man kept up a stream
of shouts and oaths till he fell asleep, snoring.

Rose scarcely registered anything of what went on
around her. She was in a state of icy panic. She had
never been to London before and she did not know
what to expect. She had been in the bus half an hour
before she realised she had not even brought Helen
Maclaren's address with her. It did not matter, she told
herself defiantly. She hadn't really been going to look
Helen up, anyhow. Not in her present abject state. But
what was she actually going to do when the bus reached
its destination? She had half a crown and a few coppers
in her purse. Although she intended to find work, you
did not walk out of the bus station and into a job, just
like that.

She did what she had always done when she found
herself in trouble, wrapped herself in a kind of mental
cocoon and let the world roll over her. Even if she did
nothing herself, things would happen to her. God
would dictate her course. Part of her mind greeted her
Maker coldly: hello, Stranger, where have You been
when I needed You? She knew this was wicked and
irreverent, but He would have to forgive her or not. She
was very far gone in her desperation, knowing she had

acted neither sensibly nor wisely. Why, why, why had she done it? But flight had seemed imperative, before she was shoved into the mould of victim. There was some determination to prove herself, deep down there in her mind. How, though, with a baby tucked away in her stomach? Rose took out some bread and marge she had wrapped in a paper bag and ate it, while the main contents of the bus disgorged themselves into a Lockerbie cafe during a refreshment stop. The woman with the baby remained seated and produced a Thermos full of tea. Hearing dry sobs from next to her, she offered some to Rose.

'Are you going down to London for a job?' she asked Rose kindly.

'No. I'm going down to marry my boyfriend. We're having a big white wedding.' Rose never knew where these occasional tall stories emanated from – she only knew that in times of stress she did revert to a child-like embroidery of the truth, for which she usually felt immediately guilty.

'Is he an Englishman, then?' demanded the woman suspiciously.

'Yes. He's a war hero and his father has a big estate in the Cotswolds.' (Please, Helen, forgive me for borrowing Johnnie Dignam just this once.)

'Oh, aye?' said Rose's fellow-traveller cynically. 'And I'm married to Ronald Colman!'

She invited Rose to smile along with her, delved into a large oilcloth bag and produced a bar of chocolate, which she shared, then presently dumped the satin-bonneted infant on Rose's lap while she disappeared in search of what she called a lavvy, while the vehicle was still stationary.

Rose didn't care whether the woman believed her or not. She stared into the baby's face and curious, considering little currant eyes stared back at her through folds of rose-pink flesh. Let happen what will happen. Through her desperation and tiredness rose a spindly thread of hope, of realisation that she still had a chance to salvage some image of herself she could live with.

Eight

Helen Maclaren looked at the image of herself in the window of Fenwick's, in Bond Street. She would have to do something soon about the way she looked. The tatty, light brown tweed coat with its big military-style revers and the flat, wedge-heeled shoes looked depressingly provincial. She lusted after a fox-fur cape and a tilted pillbox fox fur hat, for black suede shoes as dark and sooty as the back of the grate at home and for a jade cigarette holder, except that she did not smoke. She wanted the beginnings of sophistication, a dippy, swaggering walk, a blasé way of talking that would bring men up short, admiration in their startled eyes. She would soon have enough for a new suit, at least, for Hugh Latimer had squeezed a minuscule rise for her out of his stringent purse. She was tempted by blouses, but resisted. She was going to have to be very calculating and careful with her wardrobe, building it up piece by matching piece and it made more sense to wait for the suit and then match up the accessories.

She strolled up the street, enjoying what it could even then put forth in the way of luxuries in its window displays during this age of austerity and her mind swung back to the letter she had received from her mother that morning. So Rose Cassidy was in London, too. That must have caused a flutter in the dovecotes! Her mother, not having any notion of the size and scale of the capital, had suggested she keep an eye open for her. Some hope! But she worried away at what might befall Rose, as a dog might worry at an unsatisfactory bone. She wouldn't get a job if the baby was beginning to show. Or she might get a kitchen job and Helen hated to think of her being exploited in some bleak milk bar or doughnut parlour.

Supposing she did see her? Supposing Rose came looking for her? It didn't seem likely, for Rose would know she would try to persuade her either to go back home or to get in touch with Frankie, and it was clear Rose had no mind to do either.

She dragged herself, a shade unwillingly, back to Bloomsbury and the afternoon's typing. Something, other than the Rose question, some unconscious reservation or burden, was nibbling at her concentration, eating away at her sense of ease with herself. She felt dimly it was to do with Johnnie and her inability to share the stresses he was feeling. But at least she would be seeing him this evening. He had written saying how much he wanted to be with her again, and more passionate words in an intimate vein that had somehow disturbed rather than reassured her, for it was as though he was using their love as a kind of barrier, a building up – but against what? She did not know what was going on down at Knoleberry and that was the key to the whole thing. To what irked her. What sent her down to *Spectrum*'s poky cloakroom four times that afternoon, and made her peek nervously through the office window as though seeking some kind of telegraphed message from the leaves of the plane tree outside, and rendered her fingers clumsy so that precious sheets of typing paper were scrunched and thrown in the direction of the waste paper basket. Missed again! Hugh Latimer came out from his cubby-hole and barked at her for taking too long over re-typing a messy short manuscript. Seeing her forlorn young face, he ordered her, 'Make us some tea, for God's sake, and never mind the googie-eyed look.' The afternoon wore on with a gale blowing up and rain obfuscating the street lights. At five she visited the cloakroom again, put on her make-up and combed her hair. She had a fringe now she lived by herself: her mother had condemned them as frivolous and tarty.

He was always waiting for her underneath the same lamppost at five-thirty, but tonight he had not arrived. Ten minutes later, Hugh Latimer locked up the office and hurried past her, with a curt 'Is he not here yet?' and a sketchy tip of his hat. It had been a frustrating day for both of them and no doubt he couldn't wait to get home to his gin and tonic.

She tightened the belt of her plastic raincoat and peered up the street from under the dripping brim of her umbrella. What could be keeping him? A small voice inside her was already saying, 'I told you. I told you something was going wrong. Don't say I didn't warn you,' but still she peered into the rain and willed his rangy figure into view. By six o'clock she knew he would not turn up. He was never late: it was a joke between them that she was mildly erratic about time but he was congenitally punctual. She stood, past feeling cold or damp, until six-thirty. She got to know the contour of the plane tree like a sister. She saw couples come and go from the brasserie near the office. She watched the pile of evening papers, *Star*, *News*, *Standard*, dwindle and dissipate and the crowds in the street thin and evaporate till Bloomsbury London reasserted itself, calling up thin ghosts of the past, the rattle of phantom cabs, voices of typists who had come and gone, and lovers fled away.

The letter was waiting for her when she finally got home. By this time her fine hair was plastered to her head like a dark hood, the soles of her shoes had turned to cardboard. But she looked at the typed envelope with a fierce attentiveness and kept looking at it as she dried herself and divested herself of her wet clothing. The gas fire plopped out a small accommodating warmth and thus encouraged, she even managed to put the kettle on, make some toast and poach an egg before she tore the envelope open.

By then she knew there was some connection between Johnnie's non-appearance and the letter, for she had spotted the St John's Wood postmark and the only person she knew of who lived there was Johnnie's therapist, Dr Bering. It had been posted that morning and delivered, presumably, by the four o'clock post. She checked the signature first. It *was* from Dr Bering. She congratulated herself on her perspicacity. Anything to stop her reading the contents. She ate the egg on toast and drank a cup of tea and still she did not read the letter itself, but the moment could not be put off forever.

'Dear Miss Maclaren,' she read at last, 'I hope this reaches you before you keep our appointment with my client, for he will be unavoidably detained, for which he sends his sincere apologies.

'Can you ring my secretary and make an appointment to come and see me? There is a matter of some urgency which we should discuss.'

What matter? And why no explanation from Johnnie? Was he ill? She tossed and turned while the questions rolled inexorably through her mind, unanswered, and in the morning she waited till Hugh had gone out and used the office phone to call Bering's secretary. He would see her at two that very day, if that was what she wished. It was. Now all she had to do was persuade Hugh to let her have a later lunch hour and that she would work late if she had to extend it. 'Go ahead,' he agreed, 'but don't make a habit of it.'

Bering was a small, neat man, not dark as she had imagined him, but fair, with gold-rimmed spectacles and a welcoming, almost fussing manner. He chafed her cold hands between his and told his secretary to bring them coffee and biscuits.

'Now, Miss Maclaren,' he began without preamble, 'I can see you are a very sensible and well balanced young lady and that I shall be able to be completely straightforward with you.

'My clients have asked me to get in touch with you –'

'Your clients?' she intervened. 'Do you mean Johnnie himself –?'

'Johnnie, as you call him – Mr John Dignam and his father, Sir Bertram. There is no way of wrapping this up and making it palatable for you, I am afraid. Your friend Johnnie has been living with an intolerable situation for some time, one that is hindering his prospects of recovery.'

'Then tell me what it is,' she said stonily.

'He was married to Miss Simonette Hawkes on his return from Germany four months ago.'

'I don't believe you.' If time had stopped, why did she hear the tick of the pendulum clock so clearly?

'Why would I lie to you?' Bering asked gently. 'This is not pleasant for me, Miss Maclaren, I assure you.' He handed her a large, white, folded handkerchief. 'He says his father arranged the ceremony. He, Johnnie, was convinced at that point he was going to die and he had misbegotten notions of saving the estate at least. I should not tell you this, but I will. He and Simonette are not living together as man and wife – she went off to see relatives in America and to give him time to sort himself out. She is an admirable young woman, not spoiled by wealth.'

'He loves *me*.' She made the bare incontrovertible statement while the tears rolled down her cheeks.

Bering nodded.

'The fact remains, he is married and his wife does not wish to divorce him. He has dug himself a pit and only you can help him climb out of it, I am afraid. In a strange way, he is a victim of his class. You can draw a line under your relationship, not see him again. His father has offered you some kind of financial settlement –'

She threw the handkerchief down, her eyes blazing.

'Me? Take money? Did Johnnie think *that* – that I would take *money* from him?' She spat the words out as though they scalded her tongue and she got up with a precipitate movement, clutching her handbag as though it were clothes about nakedness.

'Now, now.' The therapist beat down the air with placatory gestures. 'It was mainly his father who put forward this offer. He is a powerful man, as Johnnie knows. You must make allowances for him. He has seen his only son suffer the most awful agonies of conscience, about what he has done not only to his wife but to you. I cannot put it strongly enough, Miss Maclaren. My client is not going to be able to rebuild his life, even to make any sort of recovery, unless he makes some kind of decision and sticks to it. He is a man of strong moral principles who has seen how little these can affect matters of the heart. In the circumstances, what do *you* think is best for him? If you love him, I would think this is what would guide you.'

'I won't see him again.' She shook her head with a sharp, incisive, movement. For a moment, her tortured gaze connected with that of the doctor and he was the first to look away. 'But you can tell him, as far as money is concerned, I am surprised at him. I am a Maclaren, and I am a Scot, and I have my dignity. Class or no class, does he not know that?'

'I am sure he does,' said the little doctor, quietly. He

held out a hand. 'But we are, most of us, capable of loving more than once. Remember that. This has not been easy for me, you understand. I did it to help my client. If you wish to come and see me, just to talk, at any time, feel free. It has been a pleasure to meet you.'

She drew herself up. It was funny. She had been waiting ever since she came to London to feel grown up. Now she did. If you kept your dignity, that was the secret. That was what earned you a place. She was not just grown up, but quite cold, and she was certain the feeling would be permanent. She shook the man's hand without feeling any contact. Movement was like swimming. She swam out of the consulting room and into the bitter afternoon.

That first night, Rose Cassidy had slept fitfully at the bus station. At one point a policeman came up to her and urged her to move on. 'Someone's coming for me,' she lied to him. He sat down beside her, a big, red-faced, kindly man and said, 'There are men called pimps who'll come up to you and try to get you into a wicked way of life. Now be a good girl and get yourself out of here. Back where you belong would be best.'

She wandered next into Victoria Station and there, sure enough, a swarthy, greasy-looking man approached with blandishments about her beauty and invitations to go along with him, couched in barely comprehensible broken English. She had been very frightened then and after a cup of tea and a bun at the refreshment counter had walked at dawn through the empty streets of Pimlico, noting the odd tramp in shop doorways, cats skulking in basements, the occasional night worker making for home and sleep.

She thought afterwards that some strange protective mechanism had prevented her from succumbing to the real terror of her situation that first day. She had suddenly come on Buckingham Palace and then a place she knew later to be Green Park, where for a while she sat and watched the world go by, trying to gather her scattered wits. For a time she was seduced by the glamour of the scene around her: nannies wheeling babies in big, deep-bottomed prams, girls in capes and saucer hats and veiled bowlers and well pressed suits rushing to their shops and offices, upright men in pinstripes with preoccupied looks, the whole charivari was like a book coming alive before her eyes. But then it came to her, how foreign and uncaring they looked, for not one glance was cast in her direction and she began to shake with the sensation of scarcely being there at all, of not mattering to anyone and to her consternation she began to weep and could not stop.

'What's up, luv?' The woman standing before her was dressed in a grey fur coat, tan suede boots and a silk scarf over peroxide blonde hair. She had a coarse but kindly, heavily made-up face and a large mouth with prominent teeth and held on a lead a snowy white miniature poodle with a pom-pom at the end of its tail.

'Nothing.' Rose turned her face away.

'Oh, come on, somethin's up. You run away from home?'

Beggars couldn't be choosers. That's what her mother always said and Rose suddenly found she had no option but to confide in the concerned face next to hers on the park bench.

'My name's Patricia,' the woman said. 'I'm from Liverpool. You lookin' for a job? I can use a maid. You can come with me now and no questions asked.'

She went. They walked along Piccadilly, Patricia talking brightly and companionably about what had been blitzed, what had been miraculously spared, and then along a street off Shaftesbury Avenue till they were into the very heart of Soho. There, up narrow stairs above an Italian restaurant and next door to a kind of makeshift 'revue theatre', was Patricia's flat. It was unlike any home Rose had ever seen before – full of flounced curtains, frilly cushions, artificial flowers and the smell of talcum powder. Rose drew in her breath in admiration.

Her own little room was above the flounces and furbelows and was by contrast plain and colourless. But she could do it up, couldn't she? She demurred a little when Patricia handed over her maid's uniform. Her father had often insisted she could do worse than go into service, but she had never really countenanced it till now and the skimpy black dress and frilly cap and apron brought home the indignity of her position. And how could Patricia afford a maid, a single woman like her with no visible means of support?

Her first job was to go down to the street markets and little shops and do the shopping. It was an eye-opener: Patricia could afford the best that Berwick Street Market had on offer. She had to cook that first evening, too, and managed fish and chips without too much trouble.

The first of Patricia's callers came that evening, a gentleman in pinstripes like those she'd seen in the park that morning. Patricia warned her that when she had guests, Rose was to let them in then keep out of the way in her own room, where she could get on with some sewing and ironing.

It did not take her very long to comprehend what Patricia's trade was. It filled her with a terrible sadness more than anything else. But her little room above the bustle of the streets and markets was her keep and bastion. She could not relinquish it. She was eating better than she had ever done in her life. Patricia had said in her casual way she might even be able to keep the baby when she had it. Patricia could be harsh and impatient at times, but at other times she told her of her life in vaudeville when she had been a dancer and about her husband who had been a fire-eater and had been cruel to her. After such confidences they drank cocoa together and exchanged confidences about their families. In some ways, Rose realised, she was mothering Patricia the way she had mothered Theresa, Ann-Marie, Kathleen, Hugh and Dermid at home. And little Bernadette, of sacred memory. When she told Patricia about Bernadette, her employer cried and mascara ran all down her painted cheeks. The memory of that made Rose iron Patricia's underwear and her nighties and negligees, with a degree of care and attention, and made her diligent about cleaning the stairs and polishing the brasses. It was all a long way from Glasgow and what the neighbours said, but daily Rose grew to love the streets of Soho more and to know where to buy what and even to distinguish which Italian cousin was who in the restaurant downstairs. She could go to the pictures in Leicester Square and gaze at the hats in Galeries Lafayette in Regent Street and buy violets from the woman on the steps of the Eros statue at Piccadilly Circus. As her stomach grew larger the traders were kind to her and slipped an apple or strawberry into her hand, winking. She did not think of the baby as real. Yet. But sometimes in stores or cafes she would see a man in naval uniform and wait for him to turn his head, hoping it might be Frankie Aarensen. Her baby's father. It never was.

Nine

'You have a visitor.' Mrs Pascali was out of breath from climbing the stairs to Helen's room. 'You know I don't like tenants to have visitors but he has come from Scotland. You want him to come up?'

'What is he like?'

'I will send him up,' decided Mrs Pascali. 'Then you see.' She didn't know what had got into her young tenant these days, so listless and unlike herself. She had quite taken to the young man on her doorstep, though she could not understand much he said through the impenetrable Glasgow accent.

'Brendan!' Helen's voice lightened in surprise and welcome. 'What brings you here?' She dragged him in off the landing and they shook hands a little clumsily. She took his raincoat while he stared round the bed-sitter. There was a Topolski print of Churchill and Attlee on the wall above the gas fire, a number of new books and periodicals scattered about the room and a sense of reading and browsing that made him feel at home.

'It's nice here,' he approved. He strode to the window and looked out at the view of Hyde Park. 'And an expensive view as well. You've fallen on your feet, girl.'

'Coffee?' she offered. Then the penny dropped. 'You've come to look for Rose?'

He nodded. 'I'll do what I can. But I think it's

hopeless. I'm down for an interview, too. For a trade union secretaryship. I've had enough of Glasgow.'

'But your parents?' she said quickly.

'They're going back to Ireland for a spell. My mother's been told her liver's in a bad way. What do you expect?' He looked at her, baffled, proud, intransigent. 'I've had enough,' he repeated. 'Maybe I need a new challenge. Something like that.'

'Well, it's good to see you.' She stated this with a calculated reservation in her voice, careful he should not get the wrong idea. She poured the coffee. 'Sugar?'

He held the cup in his big but well shaped hands. It was funny seeing him there, so much a part of her old life. She waited with trepidation for his next question.

'And you and Johnnie Dignam – how is it going? Is he keeping better? Do you manage to see something of him?' The questions were all posed in a straightforward, unequivocal fashion. Friend to friend. He was totally unprepared for what came next.

'I don't see him.' She had always been able to summon up a sharp, cutting tone, even as a little girl. It had provoked dozens of rows between her and Rose when they were at the hair-tugging stage. 'Who do you think you are?' Rose had always demanded, furiously.

'Why is that?'

'*My* business,' she said, but a little more gently. He noticed suddenly how thin she was, how the hip-bones jutted and the face had new angularity. Her hair did not have its usual stunning gloss. It looked somehow faded. 'I don't want to talk about it,' she insisted. 'Please.'

'O.K. That's fair enough. Do you like your job?'

She nodded fiercely and he saw something that might have been the fraction of a tear fly out and away from an eye. She wrapped her arms around her as though she were cold, although the afternoon was mild. He grew impatient with his own need to get up and hug her, touch her. It was clear she didn't want any man within a hundred miles of her. He knew her well enough to read her.

'The job's great.' She turned and managed a smile. 'I get to do quite a bit of writing. And meeting people. Names, you know.'

'The literati?'

She laughed. God, she was thin. 'You would be surprised at how dusty and down-at-heel some of them are.'

'They don't bother about how they look?'

'No. Not a lot.'

He shook himself like a young dog. 'God, it'll be great to live down here and get that sense of – freedom.'

'You never used to think like that. You had a go at me for leaving.'

'I hope I get the job.'

'I hope you get it too.'

'Then we'll be able to see something of each other.'

She let that one lie, conspicuously unanswered. Well, he shouldn't have pushed his luck.

'Have you tried the usual channels? To track down Rose? The police? The Salvation Army?'

He nodded. 'Where should I look now?'

'I've no idea. They say if you stand outside Swan and Edgar at Piccadilly, sooner or later you'll see someone you know.' She smiled thinly at the fatuity of this.

'I thought I'd try some Catholic hostels. Irish societies. Churches. That sort of thing.'

'Poor Rose. I hope she hasn't –' She stopped herself.

'Done anything silly?' He shook his head. 'She wouldn't. But she needs help. And the letters have been coming in from Frankie Aarensen. My mother opens them, without compunction. They all say when is she coming to Chicago.'

'What a mess, eh?' she postulated and he knew she wasn't only talking about his sister Rose.

That day, as he left, she noticed how shabby his navy raincoat was. Not genteel shabby or expensive shabby like Hugh Latimer's clothes. But poor shabby, ill-fitting, cheap, like everything he wore. His white shirt-cuffs were always too long and so got grimy too quickly and the collars turned up at the corners where the little cellulose stiffeners worked their way through the material.

She could not identify the feeling this roused in her. It was strong and painful, but whether it was pity or anger she was not sure. Her feelings were a minefield to her these days and she never knew what would cause them to blow up, sometimes disproportionately to the situation. Hugh Latimer was forever beating down the air with conciliatory gestures, telling her he had not meant to offend, usually over some trifle. His generous toleration of her ill-temper filled her with guilty ire.

She was not sure at that point how she could proceed with her life without Johnnie. It was like a death. She came home each night and wept storms of tears that left her eyes faded and red-rimmed and her nose feeling as though she suffered a permanent cold. Her whole body felt cold and especially her hands and feet, as though only Johnnie's presence would warm her back to life.

And yet she could not allow herself the luxury of summoning up his presence in her mind. When she did, it was as though he was trying to come forward through a kind of mist, his hands held out towards her, open-cupped and exculpatory. Yet she despised this on-coming figure, for what he had done could never be forgiven, for whatever reason. She could understand why he did not come to her himself to tell her about his marriage. Cowardice she could understand. But he was removed from the landscape of her life so totally it was worse than a bereavement. For a while she had no compass, barely knew how to pass the bread to her

mouth or go down the stairs and out to work each
morning. And he must have known he had brought her
to such a pass.

She hung on therefore to the feeling that Brendan had
engendered and pondered it as she caught the tube in
the days to come. Who had used the phrase the Great
Unwashed? Undoubtedly that was where Brendan and
she came from: well, perhaps she had been poised for a
great part of her life on the edge, one of the Partially
Washed, the Marginally Clean, the Occasional Bathers.

Part of her new life was bathing nightly but at home
there had never been a bath, just a jawbox in the kitchen,
a sink, and family hygiene a matter of carefully managed
discretion. The men washed – 'sluiced' was what her
father called it – in the morning before the women
turned their faces from the wall. She and her mother
snatched quiet times to conduct piecemeal sponging of
their persons, keeping an elderly chipped enamel basin
for weekly immersion of the feet. There was no great
difference between the washing practices of Cassidys and
themselves – just that there were so many more Cassidys
and therefore fewer opportunities for privacy.

She made her mind up that next time she saw Brendan
she would give a delicate discourse on metropolitan
manners and the need for a new suit. In some ways she
didn't want to change him at all – he had been perfectly
all right against the background of the close – but if he
wanted to get on he would have to dispose of that rural
Irish relic, the white silk muffler, get some new white
nylon shirts, a nice double-breasted suit and have his hair
cut more regularly. Manners makyth man, she would
say, and he wanted to get on, didn't he? And did she want
him to get on? Why not? They were both going to have to
get in there and fight for a place, right? Fight with
whatever weapons came to hand.

This new brusqueness and anger in her was the only

antidote that worked against her harrowing grief. She had no doubt it was her humble status, her lack of money or position, that had come between her and Johnnie. Well, there was no Johnnie in her life any more so she would replace him with hard work and ambition. She would become somebody to be reckoned with and if Brendan got this job and moved south she would back him up to the hilt. It would be marvellous to have a friend to talk to, someone to exchange ideas with, someone in whom she could confide. She was very confident she could keep the relationship between herself and Brendan that of friendship. Any relationships she had in the future would be dictated entirely by *her* wishes.

It was only her basic good health that carried her through at this time. She ate sketchily, slept poorly, read too much, cried a good deal, was erratic in her moods.

If only she could get rid of this pale supplicatory ghost that was Johnnie. The time did come when she could examine him a little more closely without her emotions splintering and running all over the place. She faced the fact that although she had known him well, she had not known him well enough.

There must have been in him – maybe from childhood – this germ of betrayal – maybe the same one that had made his odious father flirt with the Nazis in prewar Germany. Maybe there was in him a weakness her love had refused to let her see. It was strange, though. Despite her suffering, she could not totally condemn him. She knew that the ghost in her mind was one she had set up herself and one that would remain there till, at some far distant point in time, she found some nub, some secret, some understanding or forgiveness. Johnnie would never go away. Her life would have to flow past and round him, but his significance was granite.

'What's the matter? Do you think the baby's coming?'

Patricia seldom climbed the narrow stairs to Rose's attic room, but Rose had not been in evidence all day and Patricia wanted supper. She was already aggrieved that she had had to go out herself and do the shopping. The streets were piled high with snow, like great walls, on the edge of the pavements and candles guttered in the shops because coal wasn't getting through to the power stations. Plenty of other employers would have told Rose to go, especially at this advanced stage in her pregnancy, but mostly she was reliable and Patricia could not bring herself to be that hard. She gazed down at Rose, wrapped in her eiderdown quilt and squatting as close to her tiny gas fire as she could get. The gas had also been cut and the weak guttering flames scarcely registered. The room was perishing, but there was no help for it. The whole country was without light or heat for most of the day.

Rose said nothing. A tear squeezed itself down one cheek. She looked what she was, a young, frightened girl. 'I want my mother,' she admitted. Patricia bit her lip. 'Well, she's not here,' she said, but rallyingly. 'You'll need to do without your mammy. But I'm here. Do you want me to get the midwife?'

A kind of shuddering went through Rose and ended in a groan. Patricia went back down the narrow stairs towards the telephone.

Rose had prepared her bed as she had seen her mother do it back home, protecting the mattress with newspaper and brown paper with clean sheets on top. She climbed into it now, giving herself up to some powerful contractions. The lights had still not come back on by the time the midwife arrived and Patricia lit two candles – they were also scarce – and placed them as strategically as possible. Maria from the Italian restaurant downstairs, the same age as Rose and with whom she had made friends, came up to give some moral support.

'Best get it over with, eh?' she suggested. 'Then you

and me can go out and get ourselves a good time.'

'What, with a baby?' Rose managed a bit of a smile, but she liked Maria and was glad to have her there. She was a very uncomplicated, generous and giving kind of girl, quite different from Helen Maclaren and her moralistic attitudes to everything. Not that it wouldn't be nice to see Helen again. Helen. Or Brendan. Or her mother. Or Theresa. Anybody from home. Rose's smile dwindled and turned into a sob.

'*Oi*,' said Maria. 'Can't have that. What about another hot-water bottle?' She filled one from a small kettle that had been heating on a ramshackle primus stove and pushed it under the bedclothes. 'We're going dancing, ain't we, soon as you get your figure back? My mum'll look after the baby. We'll go to the Hammersmith Palais. You always said you wanted to go there. You like dancing, don't you? You said so.'

Rose nodded and clung on to Maria's convenient hand. Underneath the waves of pain she could suddenly see Green's Playhouse back home as plain as could be: she and Helen rushing towards it from work, decked out in their floral dresses, fixing their hair combs and their lipstick on the swaying tram.

And very clearly she saw Frankie Aarensen as she had not remembered him for months – his fair hair, his broad snub nose, the suggestion of freckles, the serious eyes. She could have been having this baby in Chicago with Frankie beside her, if she hadn't behaved like a total idiot. She still couldn't fathom what had made her come to London, unless she owned up to a childish, furious reaction to having the baby, that was all mixed up with what she had seen her own mother suffer. And now the fat was in the fire, she wouldn't be able to get in touch with Frankie, he would be too angry at her behaviour. And how would she explain that she was maid to a prostitute, that she had met others 'on the game' and the men who managed them and preyed on them?

She had never done anything herself she need be ashamed of: Maria had pointed that out to her. She and Maria had gone to church at Christmas and when they were lighting candles she had broken down and Maria had said the Blessed Mary forgave her. 'Judge not,' Maria had said. Maybe Patricia and the others like her had no option, their natures being what they were. Maria had said Rose was different. Rose was like her. They lived among people who were wrong 'uns but that did not mean they were bad. She had told Maria about Frankie and Maria had said she should write to him and tell him everything. But what she had done was push the thought of Frankie away from her. She still did. She was still angry he had given her the baby. She still wanted to dance and have a good time and here she was going to be with a baby to care for and feed and accommodate. It was funny that now in the middle of the pains she should see him, Frankie, so clearly, and remember what his strong body had been like and how his voice had sounded and how he had always brought her things.

'I want Frankie,' she said now, clearly, the sweat standing out on her brow. She had been in labour an awful long time and she was getting so tired. 'I want Frankie or Brendan or somebody,' she said and then she seemed to be straining out of her skin, the pain was so big. Maria wasn't smiling at her any more. What was bothering Maria? Something was.

'What's bothering you, Maria?' she shouted. 'It's not you that's having the baby.'

The midwife came and examined her again and put something to her bulging, straining abdomen and said to the others, not meaning Rose to hear, though she did, through her pain and distress she heard everything with supernatural clarity: 'She's so narrow. I lost the baby's heartbeat ...' She looked solemn and judicious. 'We'll get her into hospital.'

How did they get her on the stretcher down those narrow stairs? How did they manage not to drop her, slipping and sliding over those perishing, frozen pavements? Why did Maria's face dip up and down and where was her hand? Ah, that was better. Somebody held her hand. It was the young, serious ambulance-man. Maria's face was somewhere further back, looking like something out of a church painting.

The hospital had its own generator and there was suddenly warmth and light. Despite the cold white tiles, that felt heavenly. They were wheeling her between curtained doors and she heard the word Caesarean. Oh, well, let them do what they would. She was much too tired to care. Just before she went down under the anaesthetic she saw the Playhouse again. Dancers. Music. Lights. Her body was moving and swaying despite the baby and she felt so free and light. And there was Frankie Aarensen, beseeching her to make him forget the terrors of being blown up at sea. *Dance, Rosie, dance* ...

The next thing she remembered they were telling her about her son and the priest was beaming and saying, 'When they called me I remembered your brother' and from far down the ward, as though at the wrong end of a telescope, she saw Brendan and Helen, hurrying.

That's when she learned what a close call it had been and that the priest had been called out on that bitter night, unnecessarily as it turned out, thanks be to God, to administer the Last Rites.

PART TWO

Ten

'That's her,' said Hugh Latimer, pointing to the neat, stylish figure in slacks and safari jacket in the *Tatler*. 'Simonette Dignam. She's written a book about her travels. If you're curious you can go to the reception at the Savoy.'

He turned and looked at his assistant editor with a bland sort of innocence. 'Haven't you always wanted to know what she looked like?'

'I read the blatts too.' Helen gave the photograph he was pointing out a deliberately cursory glance. 'I've seen her picture plenty of times.'

'But in the flesh –?'

'What are you? Some kind of sadist?'

'It's all history isn't it? You don't still carry a torch for the Tory Dignam, do you? Did you know he'd end up an M.P. sitting in the great shadow of his hero, Churchill?'

'I knew it was on the cards. Didn't he make some kind of speech the other day about looking after the boys coming back from Korea?' She asked this with an almost convincing display of near-indifference.

'He's obviously going to set himself up as the Tory Party's bleeding heart, then.'

'He *does* care.' Helen turned on her boss with a face that was suddenly suffused with genuine anger. 'He's been through a lot himself. It makes him sensitive to other people's troubles.'

Hugh said pacifically, 'Oh, well, I don't suppose the Labour and Liberal Parties are the only possessors of an instinct towards decency.'

He gave Helen a sidelong glance. She had been with him for nearly six years now and in that time had grown from raw young provincial into a well groomed, impressive young woman. She hadn't moved elsewhere, although there had been offers. For a while she had gone into her shell and he suspected she stayed home and read a lot. Then ambition seemed to have kindled again and she worked for him like a Trojan. There was a tacit understanding that he was training her to take over from him – *that* would be a first, a woman editor of a 'heavy' magazine! She was aware of his increasing health problems. He was more touched than he cared to admit when he realised that she probably stayed now out of loyalty. She nagged him into taking breaks, bought his chest medicines for him and even got his shoes soled for him and warmed his coat and muffler on cold days. They were neither of them people who confided a lot but they did trust one another. And although he had never heard the whole story, he knew Helen had been deeply affected when Dignam had gone off and married someone else. The woman whose photograph he had just been looking at.

Maybe he should have kept his big mouth shut. But Helen was looking sharp and good these days, writing like an angel, apparently settled in her new South London flat, and his little ploy had been in the way of a kind of test. She could show herself how far she'd come from the crushed, humiliated girl of six years ago by going to the literary reception, seeing Simonette Dignam was just an ordinary human being like herself, and then writing a review of her book that could be as nippy and wounding as she liked. She could get just a little of her own back. Hugh didn't know how women's minds worked but he surmised they were just as fallible and human as men in this respect.

No, it wasn't as trite as that, he reprimanded himself. He wanted Helen to see life only hurt if you let it. He wanted her armoured and toughened and she was certainly shaping up that way. She had a certain blithe ruthlessness at times that made him stand back and whistle. One of their contributors had referred to her the other day as the Tartan Terror. She was going to be *très formidable*, if she kept her nerve …

'Well?' he said, raising those shaggy brows.

'I can't very well go. He might be there and I certainly don't want to see him.'

'He won't be there. He's gone abroad with some Parliamentary deputation – didn't you read?'

She turned on him and pierced him with those vivid dark blue eyes.

'Hugh, you're interfering.'

'Oh, well,' he said softly. 'If you're chicken … I leave it up to you.'

She was never blasé about going to the Savoy. Her mother liked to hear about the celebrities she spotted there. She wasn't sure if a first travel book merited the size of the reception laid on in one of the rooms overlooking the Thames, but of course the family firm had done the book proud as far as production went and were obviously not reining in when it came to publicity. *Golden Dreams, Golden Cities* was laid out in serried ranks, its purple and (of course) golden cover bold and eye-catching.

There was a fulsome handout and glossy pictures of the author looking striking and adventurous. A publicity assistant buttonholed Helen and assured her she would make sure she had a word with the writer before she left. *Golden Dreams, Golden Cities* was going to be one of the notable travel books of this post-war era.

Helen took a glass of champagne and a sausage on a stick and gazed at the new celebrity surrounded by her acolytes. She was dark-haired, pretty, vivacious and wore a tight-waisted black velvet suit with a little matching Mary Queen of Scots hat. She was being arch and loud but that was probably due to nerves. To be honest, thought Helen, she looks quite – nice. Maybe I could even like her if she weren't who she was.

Grace Rapaport from the *Sunday Sentinel* said from behind Helen's shoulder: 'Nothing like marrying into the right family, is there? If you want to write books, marry a publisher.'

Helen grimaced at her friend, small, dark and professionally disillusioned. 'Maybe it's a good book.'

'You read it? It's all right, I suppose. The joins show a bit. Listen –' she drew Helen closer, her dark eyes suddenly beady and conspiratorial, 'I hear she's having an affair with a member of the Government. No, no names, no pack-drill. I get the impression it isn't a happy marriage, despite the two little boys. Why else would she travel so much?'

'The rich, you see, are not like you and me,' said Helen, automatically. Grace was a mere professional acquaintance but when they met they played this game of being characters out of *The Great Gatsby*. She hoped Grace would not notice anything – the tendency of Helen's teeth to chatter, the desperate somersaulting of her thoughts at Grace's idle gossip. She was sure her face had gone pale. Surely it showed in her face. It was all she could do to get through the next ten minutes normally.

She forsook her chance to meet the author and escaped through the hotel's back door on to the Embankment. Her legs felt tottery, as though she had just had 'flu.

All she could think of was that he was unhappy. Having seen Simonette she was sure of it, for the woman's face had not been a happy one, either. And in her cynical fashion, Grace Rapaport had surely not been far from the truth? Why would Simonette Dignam leave her husband and two little boys and travel abroad for months on end, if she had cared about a stable home life? Helen recalled what the therapist Bering had told her about Simonette going to New York right at the beginning of the marriage, supposedly to allow Johnnie time to sort out things in his desperately unsettled mind.

The thing was, having seen Simonette, a three-dimensional being instead of a vague figure conjured out of the imagination, Helen could not now deny a certain empathy. How easy could it have been for Simonette, with heavy fathers on both sides dictating her future? And she had been in love with Johnnie, he had not been able to deny that. There had been *some* rapport between Johnnie and Simonette, if not the strong and devastating emotional imbroglio between Helen herself and Johnnie.

Helen tucked Simonette's book under her arm and made for a coffee bar at the corner of Whitehall and the Embankment. There she could gather her scattered thoughts together. She should have trusted her own instincts and not gone to the reception. She blamed Hugh Latimer and his heavy-handed intervention. There were times when he behaved as though he owned her.

Just recently she had begun to think she had got the whole Johnnie business into proportion at last. It had been salutary, in a way, teaching her to keep a guard on her emotions, a kind of inoculation against falling in love. It was better just to have men friends and to put her main energies into work. She had discovered the nascent intellectual in herself and it was a brilliant revelation, what she had learned in the past few years under Hugh's tutelage, and what still remained to be uncovered. She had no reservations now about having left Scotland. She could never have had the opportunities there that she had found here – theatre, books, poetry, music, painting. 'A harp in the wind', that was what she was, said Hugh when he was in a teasing mood. She had even begun to think that the whole unhappy episode had been necessary to give her a basis for her writing life. And now this! Everything scattered, tossed in the air, brought back with the same stabbing, indignant pain. She didn't want art. She wanted Johnnie. Wanted to see him, breathe the same air.

She had undone all her security with a single rash act. Why had she not remembered what she had been like after Johnnie's marriage and Bering's intervention? The walking of the London streets? The sitting in parks? The inability to eat properly? The sheer, unmitigated misery that had almost destroyed her? If Brendan Cassidy had not been on the scene, she knew now she would have gone under. But he had taken her in hand, listened to her, bullied her, been the best friend a girl could ever have. They'd been mutually supportive, for he hadn't found London life easy at first and had depended on her a lot as confidante.

She stared into her *cappuccino* coffee now and thought that finding Rose had helped, too. That dramatic night the priest had rung Brendan and they had pelted, the two of them, into that cold, white maternity ward and seen Sean for the first time! And what a tale had followed! Rose agreeing to write to Frankie Aarensen at last and Frankie in turn being intransigent, refusing now to have anything to do with Rose because she had not let him know what was happening to her. Bruised, angry exchanges by letter and telephone. And Rose making up her mind, that was

it, she was bringing up the baby on her own. Although
the nuns had said they could find a good adoptive home
for Sean, once she had seen her son there was no way
Rose was going to part with him. And Frankie insisted
on paying maintenance and on hearing about his
progress. Sean had grown into a handsome, headstrong
little boy, like Brendan in looks if not in temperament,
and now Rose was thinking of marrying Maria's cousin,
Guido, a waiter. And who would have thought Brendan
would have fitted so well eventually into the London
scene that he had been elected a councillor in the East
End ward where he lived?

Well, Labour had swept the board at the municipal
elections – strange that, with the Conservatives so
strongly entrenched in Parliament. But Brendan was
saying Labour's turn would come round again to govern
the country, maybe sooner than the Jeremiahs in his
party thought, and with his growing political assurance
Helen knew he hoped to be adopted as a Parliamentary
candidate in the next election. He had given up his
trade union job and was a researcher at the House of
Commons, as steeped now in politics as a herring in
vinegar. She had had a modicum of success in tidying
up his image, but the Left Wing look was one of scruffy
sports jackets, suede shoes, long hair and Brendan
largely subscribed to it.

He did not care about clothes, or where he lived (his
room in Bow was large, cold, infested with papers and
pamphlets), but he luxuriated in the ability to swop
political theories, in the theatre, in country walks in
Kent or Sussex and going to Continental films with
Helen.

She had become a bit dependent on him as best
friend, there was no doubt of that. She had had one or
two flirtations, as it happened with Fleet Street
journalists, but when they had started getting serious

she had gradually backed off. Her main thought now, as she finished her coffee and stared broodingly at the mass of the Palace of Westminster through the dusty cafeteria windows, was that the best thing she could do would be tell Brendan about her indiscreet action of earlier in the day.

She needed, daft as it sounded, an ally against herself. Someone to reassure her that Johnnie Dignam was now a mere shadow figure who could never again have any significance in her life and her sighting of Simonette Dignam no more than the passing of a ship in the night.

'Why don't you marry *me*?' said Brendan. He stood under one of the leafless trees in Leicester Square, his hands outspread like a Bible Belt preacher and an equivocal smile on his face. They had been to see *M. Hulot's Holiday* and Jacques Tati had almost succeeded in taking their minds off the conversation they had had beforehand about Helen's emotional state.

'But we're friends,' she said, helplessly.

'That's all right then,' he said, his expression slipping only fractionally. 'Where shall we go to eat?'

'The Hungarian place where they dance the csardas?'

'A bit pricey, isn't it?'

'We'll go dutch, as per usual. Come on. The music's cheerful. I need the cheerful music.'

When they were in the warm, companionable restaurant, with waiters who looked as though they liked their jobs and girls in national costume flourishing be-ribboned castanets, he placed his unremittingly shabby raincoat over the back of his chair and returned doggedly to his theme. She hadn't seen him often like this: beetle-browed and determined. Except when talking politics.

'*Why* don't we marry?' he insisted. 'I think you're lonely. You need me.'

'Me? Lonely? May I remind you I have a very responsible job. I'm practically running *Spectrum*, you know.'

'I do know. But as a Liberal, middle-ground mag it has nowhere to go. Whatever Hugh Latimer may argue, there's little room for middle-ground politics at the moment.'

'That's why we're taking it more along literary lines.'

'Can you change horses like that?'

'We've got to try. That's what's so exciting.'

He waved a hand over his mouth as the hot peppery goulash threatened to burn his tongue.

'I don't mind you throwing everything into your work, as of now. But for God's sake, girl, you have to see you must get your emotional life sorted out, too. You need security. Commitment. You'll get those from me.' He rubbed a piece of French bread round the rim of his plate. 'And I'm fond of you, incidentally. Or hadn't you noticed? Nobody else would put up with a kiss on the cheek and a doorstep farewell for five long years.'

Helen stared hard at an ear-wigging waiter. 'I haven't led you up the garden path,' she said furiously. 'You know we are just friends. I'm fond of you, too. But look at the word we use. *Fond*. Is that a word for lovers?'

'Well, I'm not Johnnie Dignam. I don't use the word love and act out something else entirely.'

'I don't know what's got into you,' she protested. 'You know how much I value you. I trust you, Brendan, more than I would trust any other human being alive.'

'You're obsessed,' he said candidly.

'What would you know? I know I had a valid experience that was something special. Please, please Brendan, don't say I strung you along. That makes me so miserable.'

'I don't care to be taken for granted.'

'Eat your rice.'

'I'd rather dance.'

They got up on the minuscule dance floor and tried to fit their steps to the csardas orchestra's version of a foxtrot. In some ways it felt very comfortable and right to have him holding her. Very familiar. But not sexy. He did it in a formal sort of way that always amused her, a bit like a teenage boy at his first school dance.

She knew Brendan had never been out with any other woman. He had plenty of female acquaintances, through his work. She was pretty sure he was celibate. But that was maybe because it was easier to square their relationship with her conscience that way. She *had* made use of him. Not exactly strung him along, but taken it for granted that he would always be there to listen to her in a neutral sort of way, as though he had no feelings of his own, or rather as though all his feelings were into political fervour. She had not seen any change in their essential relationship since they had gone to night school together.

She said now, justifying herself, 'I've always listened to your theories, Brendan. Have I not always encouraged you? I don't always agree with you —'

'You mean you've always held the whip hand. And what does that make me?'

'Don't,' she pleaded. They had been over this ground before, if in more obtuse ways, but tonight she had a sense of things coming to crisis point.

She danced in silence, not knowing for once how to proceed. He was precious to her, in the way that a brother might be. You could say that they knew each other too well, that anything sexual between them would be almost incestuous. For her there *was* no sexual chemistry. Could you kindle such desire? If she began to think of Brendan as a suitor — what an old-fashioned word! — could they cross that barrier between friendship and love?

'Sorry,' said Brendan automatically. He had trodden on her foot. She looked into his closed and sullen face, thinking how presumptuous she had been to think she had the measure of him.

'Sorry,' he said, stumbling against her once more. 'Look, this is no good, is it? Let's sit down.'

Eleven

Two days later, there was a letter from Brendan awaiting her when she got home from the office. It had been a hard day. One of *Spectrum*'s regular contributors, Sydney Felder, a hard-drinking but brilliant Fleet Street journalist, had taken issue with her because she had been forced to cut his column and with uncharacteristic clumsiness had rendered, according to him, rubbish of his peerless prose.

'What can you expect from a woman?' he had said vindictively and she had heard him sounding off to Hugh Latimer long after their own exchange. (Maybe he had expected her to say yes on the frequent occasions he had tried to date her.) Then Hugh had been very preoccupied and she wondered if there was any truth in the rumour she'd picked up that offers were being made for *Spectrum*. She wouldn't face up to the fears that aroused in her. *Spectrum* was, she acknowledged, her emotional bolt-hole as well as her livelihood. But magazines on a financial knife-edge were always the subject of speculation, and surely Hugh would have said *something* had the latest rumour been true.

It was disquieting, though. As though events were conspiring to edge her out of her safe little snail-house. Although she had the reputation for giving as good as she got, encounters like that with Sydney Felder shook her hard-won confidence in herself.

Maybe it was just too hard to make your way in a profession dominated by men. Sometimes her edgy strength and courage deserted her. Men had so much going for them and stuck together when the going got rough. She couldn't even ring Brendan any more and confide her worries to him – that would be construed in future as stringing him along.

Since the night of exchange in the Hungarian restaurant, she had forced herself to drag her whole way of life, her attitudes, out into the open and examine them as honestly as possible. She could do this in a more rational way nowadays. If she was over Johnnie Dignam, maybe Brendan was right to get her thinking of sharing her life with someone else. For, she acknowledged as she cooked pasta and chopped ham and parsley to go with it, this business of coming home at night to an empty flat could lead to too much introspection.

Like a sharp kick in the ribs came the thought of Johnnie. *That* was what she should be keeping at bay and ever since the book reception at the Savoy that was what she couldn't achieve. When she woke, when she put down a book or switched off the television, when she closed her eyes at night, there he was. She found herself thinking of going to the public gallery at the House of Commons so that she could see him. She found herself wondering how he had changed. She had seen one newspaper picture of him and it was apparent he had broadened out, but only a little. She wished fervently she had kept the picture but *then*, on the day she had spotted it, she had known she would have to destroy it immediately before this very longing overtook her. If it was an obsession, God knows it was one she fought.

But if Brendan was right about obsession, could he be right about other things? Could *their* friendship deepen into something else? She tried to imagine hearing his key in the door and seeing him walk, right now, into her sitting-room, as of right. '*What sort of day have you had, dear?*' they could ask each other and the interchange would be easeful. Sometimes he would go into one of those black, Celtic moods of his, his face closing like a dark fist, but she knew how to handle them, how to joke him out of them.

And when she was feeling fragile – that was how he termed it, and it was so right, so apposite – when she was feeling fragile he was good at making the coffee hot, producing the biscuit, backing up her judgements. Yet behind were all the years of not thinking of Brendan in *that way*, for when she got to taking the scenario further, imagining him going to bed with her, it took off into something near-farcical, something she resisted and even found funny. And that would be the end of it if she laughed at him. She could not permit herself even to think about it, it would be so wounding, so bitterly wounding. You didn't do that to people you loved, even if some of the laughter is directed at yourself. Brendan, she addressed him, what we have here is a riddle wrapped in an enigma and is best left alone.

His letter said, 'Old Yeats was right, you know. Too long a sacrifice does make the heart a shade stony. I have sacrificed too many days and nights to thinking about you, my dear Helen, and to making a right kind of ass of myself. No more, no more. I suppose we shall still see each other from time to time (why not?) but forget what I said in the restaurant. You didn't string me along. I have been entirely self-deluded but it's over. Brendan.'

Good thing too, she thought angrily. At least I've let you know where you stand. But afterwards came the tears, tears for herself, tears for making Brendan suffer. He had mentioned Yeats. She took the Yeats down from her bookshelves and read the poet's words on his long and unrequited love for Maud Gonne. 'Ah, love, if you'd but turn your head, I'd know the folly of being comforted'.

She had committed that same folly of looking for comfort. So, it seemed, had Brendan. And there was no help for them. Johnnie Dignam was never going to turn his head towards her, was he? Ever.

'Helen? In here.'

Hugh Latimer's command was short, preoccupied. She left the copy she was subbing on her desk and went into his small cubby-hole of an office.

'Hugh,' she protested, 'I'm due at the printers. Can you make it brief?'

'Forget the printer.' He raised his head and she saw his eyes looked sleepless and heavy. Something moved in her chest, some premonition. 'I'll phone them and explain,' he said. 'Later.'

She waited. She had not been going to sit down, but she did. He put his arms down on the beleaguered space in front of him and then his head. She said in panic, her hand touching his arm, 'Hugh, what's wrong?'

He sat up wearily after a couple of seconds and said, 'God, I'm tired. That's all. And I've got things to tell you. Things I'd rather not say.'

'What things? No, I know what things. The magazine is being taken over.'

'How the hell did you know?'

'There were rumours. But there have been rumours before. This time I discounted them.'

'Do you know who has made the offer?'

'Some publishing conglomerate. I didn't take in the name.'

'Knoleberry House Books.'

Her bent right knee began to tremble. 'But that's — that's the Dignam outfit. I mean, Sir Bertram is the chairman. Johnnie's father.'

Latimer threw down his pencil in some relief, glad that the worst was out.

'Well, that's it. Got it in one. I've met the old buffoon. But we'll be dealing mainly with subordinates. We're pretty small beer. It's just that they've decided, in their wisdom, the time is right for the acquisition of a political mag.'

'It isn't political any more,' she said fiercely. 'You and I have made it into something else. Haven't we?' she challenged.

He did not meet her eyes. 'Whoever takes it over can turn it in any direction they like. Although I've entered a caveat that it would rather remain an arts paper. With a woman editor. With you, in fact.'

'You're leaving?' she said unbelievingly. 'Forsaking the sinking ship?'

'Did you hear what I said?' he persisted. 'I want you to be the editor. *That* is a condition of sale.'

'Where are you going?' she demanded, feeling something more than rage send her voice up the register. Hugh Latimer said nothing. They gazed at each other across his cluttered desk and she saw she had not been mistaken, he was very tired, very weary. In fact, it seemed to be taxing him to talk at all.

'Hugh,' she said, in alarm, 'are you ill? What's the matter? You must tell me. Please.'

'I'm taking a ticket of leave. For the South of France. I haven't got much option. Or much time, maybe. But I'm not complaining. I've had a good innings.'

But I know nothing about you, she wanted to scream. I know you wrote a couple of novels when you were young, and turned out some tolerable verse — that's how you described it — but I don't know what made you afraid of women, and careless with your health, and drove you to drink more than was good for you.

'I can't work here without you,' she said, dully.

He picked his pencil up, threw it down again, fiddled with an elastic band.

'See here,' he said at last. 'I might have long enough out there in the sun. It's a place I was once very happy in. But I'll only go if I know the mag is in good hands. I've taught you all I can. I couldn't have done it if the aptitude had not been there. I think it's time women got a chance to show their paces, what with a new young queen and all that. How about it, eh, Helen?'

'I can't work with the Dignams,' she said flatly.

'The younger Dignam will have nothing to do with it. And old Sir Bertram – you'll probably be seeing him about twice yearly.'

'I don't want to see him at all.'

Hugh had a beseeching look which she found she could not meet. 'Look,' he said, 'I don't know the ins and outs of what happened between you and Johnnie Dignam. But put it behind you. Be a big grown-up girl about it.'

'How could you, Hugh? Land me in this dilemma?'

'I didn't do it. The board decided. I'm sorry, lovie. If you find in the end you can't do it, I'll give you a smashing reference.'

Possessiveness for *Spectrum* welled up in her, as he had known it would.

'I'll have to give it a try,' she owned reluctantly. 'Goddammit, I'm not handing *Spectrum* over to him.'

Now she could look at him and the stress had cleared miraculously from his expression. 'Make us a coffee, Helen,' he begged. Mostly this was left to the office junior, Kimberley, but her efforts were so dire Helen took over when the quality of the coffee mattered, as it obviously did today.

When she had placed Hugh's cup and saucer in front of him they sipped companionably, almost, she thought, like an old married couple. She put her feet up on the bars of his battered editorial chair.

'When I first came here,' said Hugh, 'it was in the twenties. The composer Erik Satie had just died and I wrote a fulsome piece about his love for the woman painter, Suzanne Valadon. My first published article. He had become a recluse and his apartment was cluttered up with love letters he had never sent. I identified with him, you see, for I was always falling in and out of love in those days.' He looked as though he was going to confide something else, but the habit of emotional reticence won. He smiled and with a little start of insight Helen knew what he must have been like – sensitive, inhibited, longing to meet someone who would understand him. How painful life could be when you were not the go-out-and-grab sort. For a moment, understanding flowed between older man and young woman that was almost like love.

'The magazine's been my life.' Hugh put down his empty cup and ran his hands through his greying thatch of hair. 'Don't let it be all of yours, Helen.'

She smiled at him without rancour. 'You mean, find myself a man.'

'I suppose so. One who'll back you up in your endeavours.'

'With you gone, Hugh, there will be no one,' she said, deliberately lightly, deliberately flirtatiously. She saw him smile and thought without cynicism: women have power, power over men. To an extent.

'There's one other thing you should know,' said Hugh. 'When I suggested your name as editor to the new board, Dignam cottoned on to who you were. He asked questions. Said his son had known you. Just that. Don't worry. I made it clear you were the best thing since sliced bread. I think he'd rather get you out but the price of my resignation is your appointment as editor. He wants a promising young fellow, name of Kenneth Fellowes, taken on as your deputy.'

'So it's locked horns, is it?' said Helen, surprised at how little the thought upset her.

'Locked horns,' Hugh agreed. 'It's up to you, lovie, to put him in his place.'

In the middle of the office shuffle came the phone call from Rose.

They did not see each other all that often because when Helen had first discovered that Rose worked for Patricia, she had been shocked to the depths of her Presbyterian soul. Even if working in London had made her more open-minded, she had still taken a stand on a better environment for bringing up Sean. And Brendan had backed her up. Rose had finally moved out of her room at Patricia's and gone to work in the kitchen of the Italian restaurant which Maria's family ran, which was where she had got to know Guido Verdi, now her husband of two months.

There was still a shadow over the girls' relationship, for Rose resented Helen's censoriousness and felt, further-more (and correctly), she did not even like Guido very much. But there was the bond of Sean, Rose's son. Helen loved the little boy unreservedly, spoiling him with presents, and because Helen loved Sean, Rose could only commend her friend's superior judgement. What had always been a somewhat prickly relationship survived because each catered to the unacknowledged, uncon-scious needs of the other – in Rose's case, she wanted approbation, and Helen wanted the feel of babies, soft-ness, even the touch of licentiousness that Soho life supplied and that was the reverse of her own celibate existence.

'Please, I want to see you,' Rose pleaded. 'Come and I'll buy you lunch.'

It was on the tip of Helen's tongue to say she was too busy, but the underlying panic in Rose's voice and the fact they hadn't seen each other since the wedding decided her otherwise.

In any case, she liked going to Soho. Liked going from the arty and scholarly ambience of Bloomsbury, where she often felt the unseen presence of Virginia Woolf, where distinguished, half-recognised faces passed you on the steps of the British Museum, to Soho, where everything assaulted the senses, coffee and cooking smells laid bare hunger, shops tempted with Continental delicacies and seedy still pictures of nudes outside the revue bars insisted on the carnal nature of man.

Looking surprisingly worldly and self-possessed, Rose waited for her in the half-lit confines of the Chinese restaurant. She had insisted on meeting there because she did not want Guido to know where she was. No doubt, Helen thought, she would be able to elicit further reasons for this surprising secrecy. Surely nothing had gone wrong already. Certainly at first glance Rose gave no hint of trouble as she kissed her friend affectionately. A delicate scent arose from her beautifully dressed dark hair and low-cut *décolletage*.

'Do you know how to use chopsticks?' Rose demanded.

Helen shook her head.

'I'll show you.' Expertly she ordered from the lengthy menu. 'We'll have a little bit of nearly everything, shall we?'

She sat back, sipping her wine, her face flushed. She was fidgety, unrelaxed, looking at the door of the restaurant as if she expected someone to walk in at any minute.

'Rose,' said Helen, beginning to share her friend's

anxiety. 'What is it? Why did we have to meet here? Not that it isn't very nice,' she added hastily.

'Guido never eats Chinese.'

'Why so worried about Guido?'

Rose took another sip of wine and forced herself to relax a little.

'I'll tell you. In a minute. But first, you tell me. Have you seen our Brendan recently?'

'He's busy,' said Helen shortly.

'He says the same about you. What's up with the pair of you?'

'Look, Brendan is just a friend I see from time to time.'

'Not often enough from his point of view.'

'Nonsense,' said Helen, briskly. She gazed into Rose's questioning face. It was no good. They could still read each other's thoughts as they had done when they were children.

'Rosie,' she explained patiently. 'Brendan can live in a pigsty and not mind. He's very other-worldly. What he needs is a nice kind motherly sort of girl, who will look after him.'

'You could,' Rose challenged.

'I don't want to mother anyone. I don't want to cook nourishing meals and cover chairs in chintz. I want to make a success of my career. Hugh Latimer thinks I can take over his chair when he retires but he's still got to convince the board. They're incredibly prejudiced against a woman, you know.'

'You're very clever,' Rose admitted grudgingly. 'That's what Brendan likes about you. You fascinate him. He sees you outstripping him. I think that's why he takes a drink nowadays, you know. He sees you getting away from him altogether.'

Helen said, shocked, 'Brendan doesn't drink. Not in the sense you mean.'

'Oh yes he does,' said Rose. 'There was whisky on his breath last time I saw him. He wasn't out of order, or anything like that. But I thought, shades of Ma and Pa. We can all go hard at it in our family.'

Helen said firmly, 'Well, I'm not taking the blame, if he chooses to be so stupid. You're his sister. You talk to him.'

Rose looked at her friend despairingly. 'He won't take it, coming from me.' She looked as though she might pursue the argument, but arguing had always resulted in Helen sticking more firmly to her own point of view. She sighed and took out a somewhat grubby little hankie, raising it to the corner of her eyes.

'O.K.' said Helen, relentless now. 'Tell me why Guido mustn't know where you are.'

'Because I have to get away from him sometimes, or I'll go mad. Did no one ever tell you about Italians? Jealousy's his middle name.'

'Even about seeing girl friends?' She saw Rose was looking increasingly upset and urged, 'It's not just that though, is it?'

'It's Sean. He shouts at him all the time. Smacks him. I know Sean can be a little devil –'

'But he's only a little boy!'

'But it's making Sean nervous. He wets the bed. He takes the other kids' money at school. What can I do, Helen? It's not that I don't love Guido. I do. But he's so possessive.'

'You'll have to stand up to him. Sean can't.'

'He wants me to work. I don't mind. He's got this restaurant in Essex in mind, he'd be great, he has a way with customers, but he doesn't earn all that much, you know.

'If I danced ... it's not stripping or anything like that. Just nice dresses, maybe a bare midriff, I wouldn't do anything I need be ashamed of and within a year I could give it up.'

'Don't,' said Helen abruptly. 'Don't do it.'

Rose said as though she hadn't heard her, 'Eat up. Lunch is on me. I got the money from Patricia – I still give her a hand, now she's retired. She still hates housework. She's moving soon, down to the Sussex coast.' She looked at Helen challengingly. 'Look, it's all right for you to be holier than thou, but people in Soho were kind to me when I needed it.'

'You don't need to dance for Guido.'

'But it pays well.'

'He shouldn't ask you to do it. In some seedy revue bar, with horrible old men ogling at you! And why do you allow him to hurt Sean?'

Rose looked sideways through the restaurant window. Two Cypriot men went by, arguing volubly. An old Chinese woman peered into her cloth shopping-bag. Rose's eyes filled up with tears. 'I didn't think he'd be like that. Sean seems to come between us.'

'Look,' Helen decided. 'Let me come back to the flat with you. I want to see Sean for myself, when he comes home from school. If I think he's suffering I'll have your husband's guts for garters. And Brendan –'

'I don't want Brendan to know anything.'

'I'll tell him if I think fit.'

'You do, and I'll never speak to you again.'

Helen glared at her friend. She understood family pride well enough, but Sean was going to come first in whatever course of action she decided.

Back in the flat, she tried to drag Rose's thoughts away from the immediate domestic situation and to get her to think of brushing up her secretarial skills. But she began to think she had lost her grip on what Rose was about. She had become more Latin than the family she had married into, her loyalty, her allegiance, all given to Guido. The more she urged Rose to stick up for herself, the more Rose excused and justified her husband.

Helen waited apprehensively for the little boy to come in from school. He was a handsome child, dark but with his American father's open, frank expression. Helen had loved him since the night of his dramatic birth. But, even allowing for the fact that he was past the stage of being cuddled and put on her knee, she wasn't prepared for the almost sullen defensiveness he exuded. He wouldn't answer her questions about how he liked school or whether he had made new friends. Only once, when he thought attention wasn't focused on him, did she catch him looking at her with a half-hopeful, almost longing expression that went straight to her heart. When she drew him to her to quiz him when Rose was out of the room, she saw a pink crescent under one eye that could have been a fading weal.

By the time she left Rose she was angry enough for action. She would ring Frankie Aarensen in Chicago. Maybe the best thing would be to lift the little chap right out of the seedy environment in which he lived. Rose wasn't going to leave Guido. Helen suspected she was in some kind of sexual thrall. Well, Sean had another parent. It was time Frankie took some responsibility for his child's existence.

'I'm coming over,' said Frankie, his voice strong and ominous. 'Just give me time to sort things out business-wise. I'll be there.'

Twelve

Helen had known their paths would cross some time, the moment Hugh had told her about Sir Bertram's involvement with *Spectrum*. How could they not, when they were both now caught up in the same circles, involved in politics and the arts? She had waited for it and schooled her heart to be brave, calm and stoic when it did. In the event, all the schooling went to the winds and every sensation in her knew a peculiar, heightened dance of pleasure in being alive. Dangerously alive. For it could not matter and it could not last.

'*Helen. After all these years.*'

'John,' she said formally. Not Johnnie. *That belonged to another time, another place*. Here and now was a wedding reception, the groom a contributor to *Spectrum*, the bride apparently a friend of the Dignam family. A committee room at the House of Commons had been set aside for the somewhat low-key post-nuptial celebrations.

'You know,' she said, the bright voice, the articulation, coming it seemed from some automatic part of herself, 'if this were Glasgow, there would be music and the dancing would go on till the wee sma' hours.'

'Now dancing,' he said, with a smile, his eyes never leaving hers for a second, 'is something I remember you do well.'

Only with you. It had taken all her will not to let the

words spill out, but the effort cost her her equilibrium. Suddenly she did not know what to do with the long gloves that she had peeled off so that she could hold the glass of champagne and the champagne itself heaved and swirled and spilled over the rim.

'Let me help you,' he pleaded. He took the glass from her while she mopped champagne from her hands and gloves. 'Let's sit down,' he said, *sotto voce*, and they moved to a small table on the periphery of the room.

'You look so – different,' he said. 'And yet so the same.' How dare he speak to her in that intimate tone, as if he had never been away?

'I am different.' And you haven't changed, she thought. You go straight to something in me that never alters, either. How is it possible, she thought dazedly, that there should be this intimacy after all that has happened, all that I have suffered because of you?

'You have certainly carried the banner for womanhood. My father tells me the whole board is prostrate before your editorial skills. Did you think when you left Scotland you would come so far, so soon?'

She was disarmed by the same old ability to tease and relax her. He was giving her time to recover. And something stronger than infatuation, obsession, overtook her. She straightened her spine and said, 'Oh yes. I knew I could do it. All one needs sometimes is the chance and Hugh Latimer gave me mine.'

It was his turn now to look discomfited. He said in a different tone, 'What about Rose? And what was her suitor called? Frankie Aarensen?'

She almost said, 'That ended in disaster, too,' but she simply shook her head. She wasn't going to disclose at this brief notice that she was waiting for Frankie to arrive to try and settle something about his child's future. She had found herself more and more reluctant to envisage the battle that might ensue there and the consequences of her own involvement. 'Rose lives in London,' she said at last, 'and is married to somebody else.'

'You haven't married?'

'No.'

A pause.

'Was I the reason for that?'

The other wedding guests seemed to be a long distance away from the little table. She felt marooned by her own sudden huge anger and the need to wound, lacerate and hurt.

'Up to a point,' she said. 'But not all men are betrayers. Not all men are skunks. Men from my own class were kind to me. I survived.'

'I would like to explain my actions to you some time. If you would let me do that.'

'Why should I bother?' she said.

'Because we may meet through my father's connection with your periodical. Because I am different. Grown up and put together at last, I hope. Because I am sorry for the way I behaved.'

'Not so sorry that you couldn't wait until a chance encounter to explain yourself. There is such a thing as Her Majesty's mail.'

'Do you think I am a skunk, then?'

'Yes. An upper-class one.'

'More of a moral coward?'

'Good definition of skunk.'

'I would like the chance to explain. We shouldn't clutter up our lives with regrets and I shall always regret running away from the situation. Which is what I did.'

'The trouble is, no explanation will suffice.'

He looked chastened and she began to feel her upper lip tremble. She saw Alistair Grainger, the groom, gaze at her questioningly from a little knot of people. She thought in a woolly, abstracted fashion she should go over and have a word with him, wish him well. But it was as though she were trapped in a kind of time capsule and there was no way out.

Johnnie was speaking again in a low, urgent voice.

'I came here tonight because I knew you would be here. I wanted to make contact again, on ground of my own choosing, because I wanted to save you embarrassment if we met up elsewhere, through my father's connection with *Spectrum*.'

She said nothing. If she concentrated very hard she could maintain the outward appearance of normality.

'Helen,' he said, 'I didn't know it would be so hard.'

'What do you mean?'

'You know.' Words seemed to be failing him. 'Look,' he said, 'do you think we could safely leave? Just slip out?'

She had been going to deny him, but instead in ten minutes found herself walking away from Westminster in her new and unsuitable stiletto heels. They walked along the Embankment, past Lambeth Bridge, towards Victoria, and he promised they would find a pub when the heels got too much.

'Takes you back,' he said regretfully. 'Doesn't it?' When she didn't reply he said, 'To the nights we went to the theatre or a concert and then walked and argued till our eyes fell shut.'

She was very conscious of him next to her and of the terrible knowledge that his power to enchant was as great as ever. When their hands brushed and he held hers, firmly, while they crossed the street, something as sweet as honey flowed through her, something she knew she must discount, nullify, but not before some transformation had partially taken place, setting her thinking, her resolution, askew.

In the pub in Victoria, all fusty leather and gilt-scrolled mirrors, she said to him, candidly, 'This won't do, Johnnie. We're only setting up trouble.'

'I want you to know something about my marriage. Simonette and I have decided to separate and there will eventually be a divorce.'

'That really is no concern of mine.'

'No, I can see that. You don't want me barging back into your life when I made such a mess of things last time. But couldn't we now be friends? Couldn't we mend some fences? I would like that more than anything.'

'I want you to know that I shall never forgive your father for offering me money. Did you know about that?'

'What money?'

'Money to leave you alone.'

'Christ,' he said. 'I never knew that. You have to believe me. I had no part in that.'

She studied his face. His look of abject misery was such that she had to believe him.

'It is unforgivable,' he said. 'I see that.'

Her smile was not really a smile at all. He took the hand that lay next to his on the pub seat and squeezing, held it. 'Don't look like that,' he begged. 'I don't know where to begin. You look so – frozen. I'm intimidated by you. I never was in the old days. I could always talk to you as though I were talking with myself.'

She took a deep, steadying breath and said, 'Well, look, O.K., when we do meet we won't fence and fight.' She withdrew her hand from his grasp. 'We'll be civilised.' She was pleased at the regaining of her composure and added, 'And I'm sorry to hear about your marriage. It won't be easy for your little boys.'

She saw a strange, unreadable expression cross his face. 'I will tell you something about my marriage. When our friendship is more firmly established.' He looked at her taut, bewildered face. 'As it will be. Mending fences is the name of the game, Helen. You will see how much I have changed since you last knew me.'

She did not know how she came to agree to see him again before they parted or, even more, how it was she asked him to dine with her in her Lambeth flat. Except that the evidence of her eyes and her intuitive intelligence told her that what he said was genuine – he did seem more solid, more stable, no longer the febrile and volatile creature who had come back from the camps in Europe in a state of semi-breakdown. She wanted to understand how the change had come about and why, if Simonette had played a part in it, the marriage was foundering. She had many reservations, and once or twice was on the point of picking up the phone and cancelling the invitation. But something about his stance stiffened her backbone and made her think it would be immature to run away from the challenge.

'You've still got the same Topolski print,' he volunteered, after she had taken his coat in the cramped hall and let him into the sitting-room. He looked round appreciatively at the walls, freshly papered in a grey Regency stripe, and at the comfortable deep armchairs and settee she had bought second-hand in Clapham. 'This is a nice flat.'

'And central,' she agreed. 'Very convenient.'

'I could do worse than take a flat in the district,' he said. 'It would be very convenient for Westminster. Meanwhile, I stay in Father's mansion flat at Victoria. It's big enough for both of us but there's always strings attached to any arrangement with Father. I'd rather be on my own.' She caught for the first time a faint moody echo from the past.

She had become quite a skilled cook and had made *coq au vin* and *tarte aux pommes*. She had put flowers, table mats and candles on the polished table by the window and urged him now to take a seat while she served up the meal. He had brought a bottle of wine which he uncorked.

'The reason I became an M.P.,' he said as they began to eat, and as though he had been rehearsing the words, formally, since they last met, 'is all to do with what happened in Germany. I felt that never again could I run away from my responsibilities. You used to find the class thing painful, Helen, didn't you, and you thought, mistakenly, that it operated with me as it did – as it does – with my father. Well, you don't go through a war and fight with chaps from the Glasgow slums without knowing who owes who. And I've decided to put my education, my heritage, if you like, at the service of those who are less articulate, less able to say what they want. We've got to give housing our priority, but after that, there are educational reforms I'd like to see –'

She said, with a painful restraint, 'Johnnie, I'm not a selection committee. You don't need to justify yourself to me. Though I expect Daddy made it easier for you to get elected.'

'I want you to understand.' The food lay, uneaten, between them, and both had put down their knives and forks. 'What I had, after the war, was classified as a breakdown. Call it what you like, it doesn't matter. What it really was, was a period of the most painful spiritual growth, when all the values I'd grown up with, the selfishness, the elitism, the snobbery, were called in question. But there were good things, too. The public school ethos is rubbished and vilified, but you learn about love and loyalty there, too. And endurance. Holding fast. I went to school with Peter Hart and we loved and trusted each other implicitly. There's goodness in people of all strata.'

'What happened to poor Peter?'

'He came off an army motor-bike. It was *instanter*. The irony of it! We came through three campaigns together, practically unscathed. And he dies when the war is won!'

She said, gently, 'Your food is getting cold.'

'This is delicious,' he said, eating. 'How kind you were to ask me here. Am I talking too much? To get back to what I was saying about breakdown, Helen: well, another aspect is that you realise how vulnerable human beings are. How frail. You saw what could happen to the human body in the camps and then I realised when I was sick and exhausted that the human personality can also be little more than a flag in the wind. God, it gives you compassion! It gives you what I can only describe as a kind of love for your fellow-man. It does. It leads you deeper and deeper into the mystery of love.'

'Does it help you to understand the breakdown of your marriage?' She knew this was a leading question and that there was a sting of bitterness in the way she said it.

He poured a little wine into her glass then some into his own. He did not answer her directly.

'Helen, darling Helen,' he said reflectively. 'Come down out of your ice kingdom. Let me get through to you. Please.'

'Do you know the Robert Frost poem?' she said. 'About fire and ice? "To say that for destruction ice, Is also great, And would suffice".'

'But that is about hate! Do you hate me, Helen?'

'I have done. Certainly I hate your father. What do you expect me to say?'

'Well, don't. I'm not worth it. Nor, after what he did, is he, though he no doubt did it with the best of intentions. His thought was to help you.'

She all but spat. 'Him I despise,' she said, flatly.

He looked at her as though sun hurt his eyes. 'You've become –' He looked away.

'What have I become?'

'Too work-orientated, perhaps. When I first knew you, all kinds of promise danced in your eyes. *You* danced. Wherever you went, you danced. Your eyes are too sad and reflective now, Helen. Wary eyes.'

'Should that surprise you?'

'I want to see the sparkle come back to them. I want to see laughter in your face. To make Helen laugh. Make Helen sparkle. I'm going to set that out as one of my aims in life. You're too thin and sober. There. I have spoken.'

She got up from the table and went into the kitchen to make the coffee. She was trembling, partly with rage at his effrontery, partly from the strength of old emotions, mostly with fright. To think she had laid her own trap. There it was, gawping in front of her.

It was as if will did not exist. Her will had been to get this long nightmare of her association with the Dignam family into perspective at last. To fight Sir Bertram if he tried to exert editorial pressure or remove her from the magazine. To put Johnnie behind her – not forget him, for she acknowledged that was not possible – but to widen the dimensions of her life so that useless regrets no longer hindered her.

She might never have had those years of discipline and sorrow. Even her treacherous body was betraying her. It seemed to loosen chains of its own making now. While she had been busy in the kitchen, he had put on a record. 'Singing in the Rain'. Banal now. Everybody knew the words. But suddenly it brought back Glasgow and the night he'd come to claim her, fighting on to the tram with a rain-sodden bouquet of roses.

'Turn it off.' She stepped back into her sitting-room with the coffee-jug.

'Don't you like it?' He came over and took the jug from her, laying it carefully on a cork mat not to mark the table. He took her in his arms and they danced.

'This is nice, isn't it?' he said. He quirked up an eyebrow, suddenly looking rakish and – what was the word she was looking for – undependable? She wanted him to look undependable. Oh, he was that all right! They danced till the record stopped and she broke away from him abruptly.

'Johnnie,' she said, pouring the coffee at last. 'I don't think I should see you again. Not in this way.'

'What way?'

'The – dancing way,' she said, exasperatedly, for he knew what she meant very well. 'You're still married, after all.'

'Not for much longer. Can't we be friends and see each other from time to time?'

'I don't think so.'

'Is it the narrow, provincial Helen talking or the one who said she wanted to be a free woman?'

'Did I say that?'

'As I remember it. You would make your own moral choices, you said. That night at Lancaster Gate.'

She wanted to protest. She wanted to cry out, 'We'll get entangled again and I might get hurt again', but none of the words came out. He remembered what she had said years ago. Just as she remembered what he had said. It made everything suddenly more valid.

'You can trust me,' he said, as if he had read her mind. 'Helen, you have to trust me. I'll spend the rest of my life making reparation, if need be.'

Thirteen

In the frilly pink negligee which Guido had bought her, Rose was washing up the breakfast things after seeing Sean off to school when the telephone rang. They only had a telephone because Guido did the ordering for the restaurant. She was still a little nervous of it and held the receiver carefully, as though it were made of glass.

'Rose, he's here.'

She began to shake and tremble. She wanted to spend a penny and to weep. She had a sense of everything crumbling.

'Rose, are you there? It's Helen. Frankie has arrived. You won't know him. He's the complete business man. Broadened out –' Helen's voice faded as the receiver was tugged out of her hand and Frankie said, 'Rose? That you? Where's my kid? At school? I want that kid, Rose. I'm taking him home with me.'

'Rose?' Helen's voice again. 'Now you know what we agreed. You have to do this for Sean, Rose –'

'He can go to his dad for a year. That's all I've agreed.' She was weeping now, her nose was running and she couldn't reach her handkerchief. 'Helen, I don't think I can go through with this.'

'You've got to,' Helen said implacably. 'Look, I've done all the dirty work. Told Guido that Sean's father had been in touch. You think that was easy? Got him to agree all this. He knows it's going to happen. Now, be

141

brave. Go down and tell Guido today's the day. Then get Sean from school and come here. I've got to get into the office soon.'

'I'm not even dressed. I'm standing here in my nightie and slippers.'

'Get dressed,' urged Helen remorselessly. 'And Rose, it's best if Guido doesn't come. He'll only send up the temperature.'

'He can't leave the restaurant anyhow.'

'Have you got Sean's things packed, as I told you? Frankie's taken care of everything else.' At the sniffing at the other end, Helen softened and said pleadingly, 'Come on, honeybun. You've really got to do this for Sean. And think how it will make things simpler for you and Guido. He'll have you to himself. He wants that, doesn't he?'

'Yes,' agreed Rose, thinly. 'I suppose he does.'

The little boy with his mother's dark hair and blue eyes stood at the door of Helen's sitting-room and fastened his eyes immediately on the man they said was his father. Rose had turned Sean out in a kind of miniature naval uniform – navy pants and brass-buttoned jacket, with a natty little cap. She was in her powder-blue wedding dress with a fox cape. She held her hand out nervously towards Frankie. Broad, sombre in a dark suit, he took it and shook it formally. 'Rose,' he said. 'How you been keeping?'

She brought Sean forward, shuffling reluctantly.

'This is your son, Frankie.'

Helen had been right when she had said Rose might not recognise him. Frankie had turned from a snub-nosed juvenile who would not have been out of place as one of the three sailors in the film *On the Town* into a broad, near-beefy, powerful-looking man with a pugnacious expression. Mix with me, the expression said, and you could be sorry.

Frankie had spent the morning regaling Helen with tales from the Chicago stockyards, where it was clear you had to be tough and aggressive on the way up. And Frankie was on the way up, he made that understood. He employed two of his own brothers. He had a house which he shared with his mother, who with the help of his sisters-in-law nearby would take care of Sean. But he had made it clear he was going to undertake the serious side of his child's upbringing himself.

When he looked at his son now, Helen had to look away, finding herself suddenly choked with abreactive tears. The big man melted from the aggressive to the tender father in a way she would not have believed had she not seen it.

'Son,' said Frankie, holding out his arms, 'did your mom tell you about this bike I've got waitin' for you in Chicago?'

'No,' said Sean, uncertainly. 'Is it a big bike?'

'She looks too thin, your friend Helen,' said Frankie, 'and a shade – I dunno – anxious.'

'She's got a responsible job,' said Rose. They were walking in St James's Park. The object of the exercise to let Sean see his parents could get on together. They were both of them aware of the irony and hypocrisy of the situation, but the heightened poignancy of it also had them by the throat. The little boy dashed forward to see the ducks and then back from time to time to take his mother by the hand.

'I wish I knew,' said Frankie, 'why you never came out to me, Rose.'

She had been intimidated by him to begin with, scarcely recognising the boy she had known in the big, bulky man who looked as though he had settled into premature middle age in the space of a few years. But as they walked the essential Frankie had come through

again, with his ready laugh and steady, shy gaze that
caught you up, helpless as burrs on a jumper.

'I couldn't cope,' she said, simply.

'It must have been tough, finding out about the baby,'
he admitted.

'I didn't want it,' she said, straightforwardly. 'I don't
want any more babies, Frankie.'

'But if only you'd told me. That was the bit that hurt. I
could have shared. That's all I wanted.'

'I didn't even want to admit I was having it. I just took
off in a haze. And when I got to London I wanted to be
my own woman, even though I was having the baby. I
don't know if you can understand that? Can you?'

He shook his head. 'All I had was this head full of
hurt and guilt. If you didn't want me, I didn't want you.
We needed somebody to knock our heads together, I
guess.' He looked at his son who was gravely assessing
the bird life at the pond's edge and pondering whether
he could snatch a stick from a smaller boy standing
nearby. 'For I didn't get rid of you as easily as all that,
Rose. I've not been able to forget you.'

She said, urgently, 'You should, after all this time.'

'I have to know. Do you feel anything at all? For me?'

She nodded, swiftly and briefly, so that he wasn't sure
whether he had seen the gesture or not.

He went on deliberately, 'Come out with me this
evening, then.'

'What do I tell Guido?' She was pale, conspiratorial.

'Tell him we've got to discuss the practicalities. Which
is true. There are a hell of a lot of practicalities. I've got
to know what Sean eats, what to read him at bedtime —'

'Guido might want to come along.'

'Talk him out of it. Tell him Helen will be there.'

'That might stop him. He doesn't care much for
Helen.' She stopped, suddenly horrified and abashed by
the turn the conversation had taken.

'You don't love him,' said Frankie, flatly. 'Not the way you loved me.'

She looked tense and agitated, turning her head to see where her son was. He had got the stick away from the other child and was trying to push a reluctant duck further out into the water. 'Sean,' she called. 'Come here! Put down that stick!'

Frankie scooped the child up in his arms. 'What about an ice-cream, sailor? Or a popsicle?'

'What's a popsicle?' inquired Sean, beginning to giggle.

'A lollipop,' said his mother, smiling. 'Your daddy is going to teach you a whole lot of new words. That'll be great, won't it, Sean?'

'I don't like Guido,' said Sean. He looked down into Frankie's face and said, 'Guido hits me sometimes.'

'Nobody's going to hit you,' said Frankie, grimly. 'Don't you worry. I'll see to that.'

She was looking tense and harassed when she met him again that night outside Marble Arch Odeon, as they had arranged. She was wearing a slightly dated-looking dress, such as she might have worn back in Glasgow, and he thought as he had then that he'd like to buy her better things, dresses which did not have droopy hems and shoes that did not crack across the front. Her face was very pink and she had plastered it with an inappropriate powder.

'Was it a problem?' he asked, referring to the matter of getting away.

'I didn't think I could make it. Then he was asked to work late shift. I just came.' She was panting in agitation.

'Will Sean be all right?'

'Maria's looking after him. He'll be O.K. with her.'

'Sure?'

'Sure.' Gradually she subsided into a normal demeanour and he was able to ask her where they should go. Dancing, he suggested. For old time's sake, eh?

'There's a place in Streatham.' She had taken a gulp at his suggestion, but accepted it.

'Streatham it is.' He hailed a taxi and she finally relaxed against its shiny black leather seat. 'This is luxury,' she said, gratefully. 'Pure luxury.' She smiled.

'Rose.' Her name came out as a reproach. He stretched out and took her hand in his and she did not draw it away.

He saw her face swimming towards him, over the shoulders of the other girls coming from the powder room and he saw how the music and lights had transformed her so that she looked exactly as she had when he first met her. Lit up from inside.

Her body began to sway almost of its own volition as they stepped on to the dance floor. And then he saw why she had worn the dress. It swirled out as she danced. She'd known, too, despite the gulp, where they would go. Her waist seemed as slim as a willow-wand. Where had he read that phrase? It suited her. She had the grace of a tree dancing in the wind. All anxiety and guilty concern had gone from her and what's more, they had deserted him too. He remembered. His body remembered. Everybody should dance, he thought. Dancing did things for you, said things for you, that words never could.

Shall we dance? Everybody was humming it that year, the music from *The King and I*. Since he'd been demobbed and sent home, he'd engaged in pursuits that were wholly masculine, his mind and senses numbed and torpid because he had become a father and yet was not a father. He'd not been able to talk to his family about it: they were people who kept their feelings buttoned up and grew alarmed if anyone showed signs of 'weakness', that was to say, emotional pain. They knew about the child, of course, and that he sent money to Britain for him, but it had been in the war, these things happened and they were just glad to have him back, taking charge of the meat-packaging firm, guaranteeing a decent living for all of them. Just as matter-of-factly, he knew, they would take his son into their midst and care for him. But they didn't want any untidy emotionalising, any agonising over what he still might or might not feel about Rose.

It came over the stoic, accepting man as he danced that Rose had been the most important thing that had ever happened to him, that she could have lifted him out and away from his family and given him the chance to develop finer feelings, to send tendrils out into the world that would not touch meat, carcases, shot deer, gaffed fish.

She had given him a son, however reluctantly, who might go to college, read books, aspire to intangible rewards that had everything to do with feeling and knowing and nothing to do with getting.

And what he felt was all to do with holding Rose in his arms, turning her into the crowd of dancers at his touch, his guidance, feeling her small hand, her waist that was as slim as a willow-wand and her fine hair like an angel's breath on his cheek.

He could feel something rise in him that was like the crush of boulders racing down a mountainside after a flood. Something powerful and primeval and terrifying. He was not in control. He had even lost the rhythm of the dance and the music was like a mad jangle in his ears.

He dragged Rose off the dance floor and into the foyer, deserted now except for the manager having a quiet cigarette.

'Get your coat,' he said, brusquely. 'We're going.'

They walked in the direction of Streatham Common.

'What's the matter?' Rose demanded.

'You should leave him,' he said savagely. 'You don't belong to him. You're the mother of my son and you belong to us, both of us. Sean and me. Not to that evil dago you've married.'

'I love him,' said Rose defiantly.

'Then why are you out with me? What sort of a tramp are you? You admitted you still had feelings for *me*. How can you – say you love *him* and say you have feelings for *me*?'

'I don't know,' she admitted wildly. 'Maybe I am a tramp. I was lonely for a long time. You need the protection of a man, if you live in Soho. He protects me.'

'Don't live in Soho.'

'You can't choose,' she cried at him. 'You can't choose everything that happens to you. You can't make it all tidy. You have to do the best you can.'

'It would have been simple enough. I would have sent you the money and you could have come to Chicago, married me in a church, and had Sean.'

'And how may more?'

'Don't you want more children?'

'You know what kids did to my mother? Even after they went back to Ireland and he knew she was sick, my father gave her another one and she died.'

'I didn't know that. Your mother died?'

'He knew the birds never sang for her after Bernadette died. That's what she used to say. "The birds have stopped singing." Yet he gave her a baby and it died and she died. Guido makes sure I won't have babies. He defies the church for me.'

'I have nothing against birth control.'

'You're not a Catholic. So it's different.'

'If you defy the church in one way, you can do it in

another. Get a divorce.'

'I can't, for God's sake. Just because I hurt you doesn't mean I do the same to Guido.'

'He abuses our child.'

'He tries to discipline Sean.'

'Is that what you call it? Discipline!'

'If we could just have some time on our own, things would get better. If you take Sean for a year –'

'I'm taking him for good, Rose. Whatever you say.'

They reached the Common. It was a moonless night and they began to track across it and as the main road with its lights receded she had a feeling of leaving the civilised world behind. Yet there was no help for it. She and Frankie had to have this conversation, had to reach some kind of accommodation. And in a kind of insistent, girlish way that went back to what they had meant to each other in Glasgow and was connected with their dancing together back in the ballroom, she wanted to reach out and – comfort was the wrong word for it. Offer him love. But it had to be of a sort that wouldn't be enough.

She said in a broken voice, 'You remember the dog you saved, Frankie? You remember Sam? Sam got killed. He ran out of the house one day and got himself run over.' She had not meant to say this. She found tears running down her cheeks. 'It wasn't my fault. Honest. I hope you'll forgive me.'

He put his arm round her and drew her to him.

'I can forgive you anything. But don't leave me. Don't work things over in your mind. Just come back to America with me and Sean. That's all.'

He tilted up her face and his lips came down on hers, his arms pinioned her arms. She spoke frantically into his kisses, 'No, Frankie. Don't. Please.'

'One kiss.' She dragged her head away. Across the dark and moonless Common not another soul to be seen. In terror, she submitted, and then for what might have been one second or ten everything went out of her head and she responded. Her hands curled in remembered tenderness on his neck.

'Oh, love,' he said. 'Oh love.'

Then she broke away and began at a stumbling run to try and reach the footpath. Car lights broke, rose, probed in the distance. She could hear his even breath as he ran after her.

He caught up with her once more, struggling to hold her, reassure her, to apologise.

'It's all right, I won't. I'm sorry.'

'You bastard,' she said softly. She brought her arms with its handbag down as hard as she could on his restraining grip and then ran blindly into the night and it seemed, for ever.

Thank God! The road was nearer than she thought! She manoeuvred to avoid a heavy bench put near the grass's edge then her foot caught something, a raised stone, and she fell headlong, her head catching the edge of the bench and killing consciousness even as she cried out.

Fourteen

'You should have kept out of it,' said Brendan furiously. 'You think you know how everybody should run their lives and you don't.'

'I did it for the best,' said Helen stubbornly. She sat, in her yellow coat, her face peaked and anxious, like a bird perched for flight. She barely had time for the scorching hot *cappuccino* coffee, in fact, for the magazine's deadline was approaching and there was final copy awaiting her urgent subbing at the office. But he had dragged her out so that their exchange would not be witnessed by Kimberley and whoever else chose to come into the office.

'Now the boy has been snatched and she might never get him back. Do you know what you've done to her?' He could barely get the words out for the weight of emotion behind them.

'I couldn't let it go on, Guido mistreating him and Rose all but shutting her eyes to it. Frankie should have waited but I can understand him panicking.' Now her own reservations about Frankie's course of action were getting to her and he saw her lower lip tremble. But he was in no mood to reassure her. He was still shocked from getting the late-night phone call from St Thomas's, which was where Frankie had taken Rose after the fall on the common which had knocked her out.

Rose was still at the hospital. She had regained consciousness but they were still keeping her in. What had happened after that was what had sent him headlong in search of Helen. Frankie, on realising that Rose was going to be all right, had gone the next morning to Sean's infant school and abstracted his son from the playground. A few hours later, they were over the Atlantic bound for Chicago. Rose had agreed to the formalities, after all.

'Look,' said Helen, 'I've got to go, Brendan. Come to the flat for supper and we'll have it out, properly. I'm just as worried about Rose as you are.'

He gave her the black-browed Jesuit look that always pulled her up short and that was the reverse of his normal, equable behaviour, but she got up before he could equivocate, leaving the money for her own coffee on the table beside him.

She made a scratch meal from eggs, cheese and ripe Conference pears for their supper. Neither was strictly aware of what they were eating, anyway, but it had been a long day for both of them and hunger made them both swallow something down. Afterwards she lay back in one of the big easy chairs and conscience jibed at him when he saw her pallor.

'You should have consulted me,' he reproached her, though his tone was now a reasoned and more gentle one. 'I could have intervened between Guido and Rose about the child.'

'She wouldn't let me ring you,' she protested. 'She didn't want you to know that side of Guido. Even with me she was guarded. But I saw what was happening to Sean for myself. I saw a big red weal just healing under his eye and I knew from his behaviour he was a frightened little boy. Maybe I was a shade importunate but you don't stop to think all that rationally when you see a child being mistreated. Frankie's never disowned his son. He's always sent money for him. I felt he should come over and size the situation up for himself. I still don't see myself as misguided.'

'Ah, well.' He threw up his hands. 'It says a lot for the state of affairs between you and me that you couldn't put me in the picture.'

'You've been offhand with me.' She could not prevent the disagreeable note of huffiness. 'Rose has noticed it, too, – your attitude towards her. No wonder she didn't ring you. You're not the Brendan either of us used to know. *And* Rose worries about your drinking.'

He got up and poured himself more coffee. She saw he was giving himself time to get his feelings under control, but also that the last point had gone home. She said, 'I hope you'll tell me neither of us needs to worry in that respect.'

'What's it to either of you?' he said, ungraciously.

'Well, speaking for myself, I don't want to see a man with all your capabilities drowning them in the whisky bottle.'

What he would have liked to have said lay between them clearer than words. He drew up his shoulders in a gesture of resignation and said brusquely, 'Never mind us, Rose is the problem. Should I persuade her to leave Guido and come and live with me? I could look for a bigger place.'

'She won't leave him.'

'She should.'

'When did women ever do what they should? She seemed to think that if they could only have a breathing space on their own, they could maybe make things work. That's why she agreed to let Frankie have Sean – it was to be only for a year, as she saw it. All that's happened is that Frankie has jumped the gun a bit – he must have thought she might change her mind, after the accident on the Common.'

'He wanted her to go with him.'

'I suppose,' she said, reflectively, 'that we'll have to let her make up her own mind.'

'She's going to miss Sean.'

'That's what worries me.'

She jumped up, thought of offering him a drink, then instead put on the kettle and offered tea. Some of the heat and anger had gone out of the situation and they were able to discuss Rose and Sean and what might happen to them more rationally. At length the conversation even turned to other things – his work, the possibility of his being adopted as Labour candidate for his East End constituency when, as seemed possible, the present incumbent was forced to take the Chiltern Hundreds due to ill-health.

'I see your Tory friend Dignam made his maiden speech the other day. The countryside's friend.' The reference, slipped in with a casual ease that did not deceive her, caught her unawares. She could feel her face give away those revealing emotions she would rather have kept to herself.

'I've seen him,' she said quickly. 'We've met up. His father is my chairman – their group took over when Hugh Latimer went.'

'It couldn't have been an easy meeting.'

'No.' She agreed with him hastily, deciding she would not tell him anything else. He gave her a long, considering look and then laughed. It had a sharp, lacerating sound. But instead of urging her to talk more about her feelings, he came and sat beside her on the settee and putting his arm around her, drew her to him and kissed her on the cheek. 'Ain't life a bugger,' he said, 'whichever way you look at it?'

She drew him gently back to their reason for meeting. 'It *is* for Rose,' she reminded him. 'We'll have to remember that.'

When she held his coat out for him when he left, she could not help noticing his shirt cuffs. They were grubbier than she had ever seen them. She pulled the right-hand cuff down and held it disdainfully between her fingers. 'Don't you ever wash them?'

'I didn't think it was too bad.'

'It's pretty bad.'

'Whisky and grubby cuffs. Is there any help for me, do you think?'

She shook her head.

Kenneth Fellowes had not exactly breezed into place as her deputy on *Spectrum*. Rather he had trickled in, only once or twice a week to begin with, as he was finishing a book of essays to a publisher's deadline. But in a quietly insidious way he had arranged the office so that his desk looked down into the deceptively country-green heart of the plane tree – Helen had taken over Hugh's cubby-hole because you could command the whole office with the door open or shut the door, and enjoy the benefits of silence – and he soon had Kimberley leaping to his soft commands and his own string of would-be contributors dropping in on a regular basis.

Helen had not been taken in by his low-key approach and soft, rather sibilant manner of speaking. He was a small, neat man with wavy brown hair growing back abundantly from a domed forehead and a neat way of putting on his folded scarf and his dark overcoat. He wore dusty suede shoes and a yellow pocket handkerchief. Yet what he said was always clear and pertinent – cutting out the fluff was how he put it – and she enjoyed the paradoxical knowledge that while he could look as prim and proper as a maiden aunt he was the father of five small children in a big bundly house in Wimbledon.

She had been long enough in London, however, to

know ambition came in many guises and Kenneth Fellowes gave off the clear scent of a young man who would not easily give up the goals he had set himself. When they had shaken hands at their first meeting both had tacitly acknowledged that a battle – a civilised, perhaps attenuated one, but a battle nevertheless, was on. Helen was surprised at how much spice it added to her daily life after Hugh.

She had wondered when their first major skirmish might occur and it happened over his editorial on Johnnie Dignam's maiden speech. It was a cleverly written piece on the postwar environment and he had skilfully brought in Johnnie Dignam's impassioned vision of a protected countryside and villages sustained by the introduction of new, small-scale cottage industries. Helen suspected the thin end of the chairman's wedge and had this view confirmed by Kenneth Fellowes. 'The old chap wants us to beat this particular drum,' he said, in his throw-away manner.

'We are not a political magazine,' said Helen. 'Nor yet a vehicle for the chairman's views as and when he feels like publicising them.'

'I think you'll find otherwise,' said Kenneth Fellowes, with all the chill mildness at his command. Helen took the offending piece out and substituted one on the future of British ballet. Then she waited for the roof to fall in. Despite everything, she had not yet met Johnnie's father.

Her head was down and she was editing a particularly dense and prolix review on a book about Greek architecture when she heard a rumble of voices and the door to her office flew open.

A handsome pink old man in a blue pin-stripe suit, his figure slightly bent over a silver-topped cane, his hair immaculately coiffed and his moustache waxed within a whisker of caricature, was gazing down at her. And smiling. Full of foreboding, she rose slowly. '*A man may smile and smile, and be a villain.*' This was Sir Bertram, Johnnie's father. The man who had offered her money. Who thought that money and class could buy anything.

'My dear lady,' said Sir Bertram. 'At last I have the pleasure of making your acquaintance. I trust this is not an inconvenient time.'

Helen wiped grimy, ink-stained fingers down her skirt. She was conscious of the fine sweat of effort lying on her cheekbones and of the need to stretch her cramped limbs. But even as she did so and shook the old man's proffered hand, the impulse of protect and defend her domain sent shock-waves down her bloodstream, rocking her back on her heels.

He did not waste much time on the formalities. With Kenneth Fellowes standing at his shoulder, he said, 'Pity about that editorial. The one young Fellowes here mentioned to me. We have to protect the countryside, you know, or we'll have Metroland all the way out to the Cotswolds. Can it go in next week?'

'I shouldn't think so.' She turned her head away from him. 'The pages are set up.'

'Have to accept some guidance, y'know.' Sir Bertram engaged her gaze and she knew she had been right – oh, a hundred times right! – not to trust that first, grand-fatherly impression. There was no kindliness there, in the blue eyes so like Johnnie's. Only a harsh, compressed judgement. 'The board is not a mere formality.'

'I was not aware the board had met.' She knew it had not. She was telling him he was not the board.

'Ha!' Sir Bertram turned away impatiently and said to Kenneth Fellowes, deliberately cutting Helen out of the discussion, 'I am sure you can take the matter up in some future article, young man. We cannot let the matter just die off. Prime your editor here on its importance.'

He was very lame, she thought, as he left. She thought

she should feel some compassion for his lameness and admiration for the straight spine that went with it, but she did not.

She thought that this was a man who would have very little compassion for anyone. Who was used to giving commands and having them carried out. How had he produced someone like Johnnie, who had won praise for his moderate and well judged Parliamentary appearance? Johnnie would make his own way in Parliament. He did not need this old ogre manipulating his way forward. She wouldn't be compromised. For Johnnie's sake as well as the magazine's independence she was not giving in. But the look Kenneth Fellowes gave her when he returned from seeing the old man into his car warned her just what she had taken on.

On her way home, she ruminated on her own intransigence. The darkened windows of the tube train gave back her image, that of a bright-haired woman in good smart clothes, with her mouth turned down. Maybe she was becoming a humourless hag. She made up her mind that Bertram Dignam would not do this to her. She put before her the magazine as she wanted it to be – as Hugh had entrusted her to make it – a magazine full of good writing and spirited insight into the arts. Sometimes she felt London stirring like a great post-war cultural giant, talents dripping from its arms like blossoms from a huge bouquet. Some of those talents got crushed, withered away. They needed to be picked up, nursed, encouraged. She believed in what she was doing. Hugh had taught her well.

She felt more than a little pleased with herself. She had acquitted herself well enough in her first encounter with Sir Bertram. Kenneth Fellowes she thought she could cope with, even partially win over, given time. She looked at her image again. It was blurry, but the mouth at least turned up.

Once home, she began, however, to be chivvied by doubts. It would not be the end of the world if she lost the job on *Spectrum*. She was sure other jobs would be open to her. But why was she thinking like this? Allowing that old man to get to her? She began to think of ringing Johnnie. He had given her his secretary's number at the House of Commons. She dialled and left a message: please ask him to ring me at this number.

It was not the telephone that rang but her doorbell. Johnnie stood there, bearing a bottle of wine. 'I was so pleased to get your message. I thought I'd come in person.' He stood in the narrow hall and grinned at her. 'I've just been waiting for the excuse.' He leaned over and kissed her on the mouth. Self-consciously, she wiped the kiss away.

She reproached herself as they walked into the sitting-room. She had undoubtedly been rash. But it wasn't any good. The graph of her happiness rose and disappeared off the paper. Useless, useless defences of remembered pain! This human being, out of all in the universe, had the power to change her day from plain to fancy. Had the power to make things well.

As though he sensed what she felt, he put the bottle down on the table and came over and took her in his arms. He tilted up her face and kissed her once again, this time seriously. He bent his right fingers and ran his knuckles down the curve of her cheek. He was moved, too, she saw that. He said, trying hard to iron the emotionalism from his voice, but not succeeding, 'I miss you such a lot.'

She asked him, confusedly, to open the wine, poured him a glass and made him sit down. He complained. 'You're a bossy little article,' and she laughed and admitted it was the case.

'I saw your father today.' She watched his face closely but he was impassive. 'He wanted to make me keep in an editorial which was mainly about your recent speech and I took a stand on principle and threw it out. Nothing personal.'

'That was brave of you.' He said it flatly. She tried to discern what it was he felt exactly.

'I'm not afraid of him.'

'I don't want to see you lose your job.'

She threw up her head. 'You don't know me if you think I'll submit to bully-boy tactics. That magazine does not belong to some ageing dilettante who comes in twice a year. Hugh Latimer let it go on three conditions: one, that it covered the middle ground in politics, on the rare occasions that politics *were* covered; two, that it supported the arts and interpreted them for a wider public; and three, that I had the final say on contents. I am the editor.'

'What about making money?'

'That is not the over-riding motive.'

'It has to come into it, Helen. I've seen the figures and they're not good. If the board pumps money into the magazine, they are entitled to a say in how it is run.'

She was silent. She had fallen into her habitual crouched and kneeling position in front of the gas fire. Now she fiddled with the knife pleats on the skirt of her grey dress.

'I want to see you make it on your own.'

'Don't you think I have done?'

'Not from where I'm sitting. It seems to me you have centuries of privilege behind you. Money. Connections. It was a good speech but your father would have you elevated to Cabinet level on the strength of it.'

'You are being ridiculous.'

She leaned on his knee. 'Maybe I am. But I and others like me came up from nothing. We are the *sans culottes*.'

Suddenly their faces were smiling into each other at the quaintness of the expression. He held her gaze, put out his hands and cupped her face. 'Darling,' he said, as though the word had just been invented. It was like the times in the front parlour of the tenement flat during the war, when she had first acknowledged the inevitability of their attraction for each other. There was really nothing that could come between them, neither class nor time nor his father, nor convention nor the thought of Simonette and even the children.

'But wait,' she said urgently. 'Johnnie, we should wait. We really should not see each other till your divorce is through.'

He put his arms gently, comfortably around her, kissing the top of her head, then held her at arm's length.

'It is asking too much,' he said, simply. 'Wait a moment.' He sprang up and put out the light, so that there was only the gas fire and the street light for company. He placed a cushion on the rug and then gently pushed her back on it.

'Tell me to go away. Now.'

It was like setting off without warning on some wild, tempestuous journey. The body came into it – of course the body came into it – but what touched were years of helpless longing, negated desires, inexpressible dreams.

The images that went through her mind were almost comically Blakean – skies rent, thunderclouds parting, torrents rending the earth. In some ways it was like being destroyed but she knew if she held on to him, clung on to him, somehow she would survive, there would be a landscape of peace after the convulsions.

Of course the body came into it. After the first coming together that was almost like a common assault, the body gently pushed all guilt, all past sadness, all betrayal to one side and watched them wither, caught up in a swift, instant flame. And then the body – her body – was like fields after summer rain, touched by a beneficent sun, made to yield after the plough and the harrow. How light, transmutable, responsive her body could be!

And then his. How was it they came to be naked? She had no memory of them taking off clothes, it must have been in the time of the tempest, when everything was churned up in the whirlwind. But his beautiful body was her teacher, bringing the senses of touch, sight, smell, taste for the first time, because there could never have been a time like this before, this was the true time, the first time, the sacrificial and the sacramental time. After this time, there would be no going back.

Fifteen

When Helen was in sober or reflective mood, she always cleaned the flat. There was something restorative about washing the kitchen floor and tidying the cupboards, something reassuring about those simple household skills like polishing and ironing. *Putting your house in order.*

And she had plenty to think about. The way in which nothing had changed. When she had first known Johnnie, he had been thin, nervous, moody. His body was harder now, more mature, but there was still something about him that made her think of a quivering young animal. There was nothing of the phlegmatic about him. Ideas, sensations, responses touched him like a harp. It was this responsiveness, this fine tuning, that evinced the longing need in her to complement it. Some men could understand women in a cerebral way and others were not slow in emotional response, but with Johnnie both reactions were there – the quick instinctive understanding and the warm reaching out. Even now, hot and grimy from her morning's effort, she could imagine his arms about her and his voice in her ear and it was like a kind of transportation, only part sexual. It was a little like a vision of what heaven might be like, when all sores and complexities have been ironed out and total understanding given. She looked back on what had happened last night with something like incredulity. Had it really been like that? A kind of madness, really. It had to be.

Last night was last night, today was today. *Today*, an insistent part of her wanted to go back to the time when Johnnie had decided not to marry her. Given that he had been very ill at the time, given that Simonette and he had been engaged to marry, given pressure from his father, the conviction lay in her, hard and incontrovertible, that nonetheless he should have held out for her.

He had promised to tell her something about his marriage when their restored relationship was more certain. So when would that be? And how could he ever convince her that the course of action which had resulted in so much pain and destructiveness had been a tenable one for him at the time? She would be a silly, gullible woman if she ignored the warning bells going off relentlessly in that part of her mind reserved for rationality and plain common sense.

Back in the same mucky old pond, she thought, with a glimmer of humour. On the one hand, knowing and loving him as though he were primeval part of me; and on the other, this gaping void that is all question and no answer.

Brendan would shake his head at her. Not that she needed him popping into her mind just now. Some nice woman would simply have to take him over, wash his shirts, answer the doorbell to the needy and inadequate. He should have been a priest, she thought, with quite unaccustomed savagery. For that's where the roots of his goodness lie, in the church he claims to disregard.

Johnnie had said he would ring her. She bathed and dressed after her exertions, one ear cocked for the telephone bell. Normally on a Saturday she did her food shopping, sometimes meeting a friend for a coffee. Today the shopping would have to wait. Hearing from Johnnie had suddenly become the only thing that mattered.

She had become so tense she slopped the coffee from cup to saucer when the phone finally burst into life.

'Darling,' he said. One word, and it was all right. Her universe juddered back into order. 'I'm sorry I'm late in ringing. But I've been making arrangements. Can you be ready in about half an hour and I'll pick you up?'

'What are we doing? Where are we going?'

'Trust me?'

'Well, yes, of course. But –'

'I'll explain when I see you.'

She stood undecided whether to wear the yellow coat with the big sleeves or change into the dark green velvet suit and black sweater. She was mildly annoyed with him that he had given no hint of what they might be doing, but since it might end with the theatre or a meal out she chose the latter. It set off her hair and pale skin quite dramatically. She took her shopping-basket because whatever they did she'd have to snatch five minutes to replenish her fridge and larder. If she kept her mind on such things as milk and cornflakes now she would not have to argue over the moral principles of taking up with Johnnie again or even listen to that pragmatic Glasgow part of her that put her down as a fool.

His car was ancient but dashing. A Daimler, she guessed, though she knew little about cars. Before he started the engine he looked at her closely, then said, 'It's bull-by-the-horns time, my love. I'm taking you down to Knoleberry to meet Father.'

She made a move as though to leave the car but he restrained her. 'I don't want to see him,' she said adamantly. 'Whatever made you think you could do this to me?'

'He rang me late late last night – he'd been trying to get me all evening. I'm very much afraid it's battle stations. He wants you out. Off the magazine.'

'And what did you tell him?'

'I told him that I intended to marry you.'

There was a silence that grew within the car till Helen felt her mind might implode. The words 'You did what?' would not come out. She simply sat staring at him till he shook her arm impatiently. 'Say something,' he implored her. 'You know that after last night it's inevitable.'

'No!' she shrieked at him. 'We haven't got to that point yet –'

'Yes we have.'

'We have to talk, to sort things out. I have to have the answers to a lot of questions. You have children, for God's sake. Don't you think about what's going to happen to them?'

'Of course I do,' he said, suddenly much grimmer. 'But if you love me, you will love my children.'

'Stop this,' she said, matching his tone. 'I do love you, you know that, but it's insane to talk as if our marriage is a *fait accompli* when you haven't even got your divorce.'

'Helen, don't be so Scotch.'

'I *am* Scotch and puritanical and I know that adultery is wrong. I'm Scotch and working-class and I think of children as too important to stuff away in some boarding-school and forget about –'

'You think God hates sinners? Well, God hates hypocrisy even more. He thinks it's just as bad to sin in your heart.'

'I won't give up the magazine.' There, it was out, her statement of intent.

'When we are married, would you want to carry on?'

'Why, of course. The magazine is what I do.'

He started the car, very deliberately. He had gone very white in his anger and she saw his mouth pulled down in a way that revealed traces of the child he had been. She ignored the softening, the giving in, taking place inside her.

'What you would do,' he said, steering out of her street, past the busy Saturday morning market, making for Putney and the road west, 'is be married to me.'

'What I would *be*,' she said, equally deliberately, 'is your wife. What I would *do* is run a magazine. I'm always going to have a career. It is my security clause.' She sought desperately for the words to explain. 'I am me, who I am, through my work. Just as you are, Johnnie. Don't you see that?'

They had driven through the London suburbs now and were out in open country, the fields tricked out in the fresh wet colours of spring. It had been some time since she had been out of London and she found herself looking for snowdrops, crocus, daffodils. Not only that, you could see sky, big rolling acres of clouds and that harsh cerulean blue that comes with March. Despite everything, she responded to the growth around them, she was host to seeds of promise and pleasure.

'About my children.' He did not take his eyes off the road ahead. She waited, her knees moving restlessly under the thick tartan rug he had spread over them. 'One of them is not mine. The elder. He is the child of Simonette and Peter. Peter Hart. Now you know why I married her when I did.'

She said nothing. She looked down at her hands and fingers, almost idly thinking: yes, he gave me this signet ring, right at the beginning. Before all these complications existed.

'I thought I was dying. I thought it was something I could do for Peter. We had been so close. Grown up together. Gone through the horrors of public school together. Two waifs sent away from home at the age of seven. Maybe that is barbaric. But we would have done anything for each other.'

'Yes,' she said. 'I remember how he came to meet me in the station that night. The first time your father tried

to put something between us. And I thought it was like
that: that he *would* do anything for you.'

He looked quickly at her and saw she was not being
ironic.

'Maybe he even loved Simonette because I did. I don't
pretend to understand. It was a quite brief affair, one
week when he had leave, then he came out to Berlin and
was killed. She was in an awful state. We both were. She
could confide only in me. The families knew nothing
about it.

'You know I wanted you. What my father argued,
about staying in my class, about keeping the estate going
through Simonette's fortune, didn't really rate with me
in the end. I ask you to believe that. At least, not to any
great extent. But I did care for her – I still do, on a
certain level – and I was devastated – quite devastated –
when Peter died. It seemed to me I had no option but to
pay a kind of debt to both of them.'

Again he drove in silence for a time, with the same set
expression.

'You can subvert your feelings to a certain extent,' he
said carefully. 'But you pay for it. As I've said, I wanted
you and when I didn't get you –'

'Did you look for me,' she asked, 'when you walked
into restaurants or the foyers of theatres?'

He smiled. 'On station platforms. I looked for girls
with red-gold hair to their shoulders. And when they
turned round and weren't you –'

'I know. I saw you a thousand times.'

'Don't say these things. It crucifies me.'

'Do you feel differently about Peter's child from how
you do about your own?'

'For Bertie? No, he and Jamie are the same to me.
That part of it has never been difficult.'

'Doesn't it matter, who inherits?'

She saw his eyelids flicker. 'There will be less and less

of that. To inherit, I mean. I think Jamie will be his own man, in any case. I hope so.'

She was gulping for air, filled with such an overwhelming recollection of desertion and desolation that the tears fell faster than she could wipe them away.

'The fact remains, you chose –' she choked on the words – 'you chose your inherited loyalties over me.'

He drove till there was a lay-by in the road then drew up and turned to face her. He handed her a handkerchief from his top pocket.

'I thought – I thought you were stronger than Simonette. I thought, if someone has to bear what comes out of this imbroglio, you were better able to bear it. You had – have strengths she will never have.'

'Such as?'

'I don't know. A positive rightness. The knowledge of where you are going.'

'I have to come to terms with that. With what I've just told you. That you put others before me. When you profess to love me.'

'I put weakness before strength. Simonette would have gone under if I hadn't offered help.'

'What do you mean?'

'She would have killed herself.'

'You can't be sure of that.'

'She said she would.'

He leaned across and took her in his arms. 'Darling, try not to let yourself get too upset. We're going to need all our gumption to tackle Father head-on. I'm not going to let him sack you. But this morning he'll have been on to the rest of the board, getting them on his side if he can.'

'How do you propose to tackle him?'

'Head-on confrontation. I can't see any other way.'

'I want to know one more thing.' She gazed at him with tears still rimming her lashes and he put out a finger and gently mopped them away.

'What's that?'

'Is your marriage really over? You say you still care for her.'

'It's over. I care for her, about her, but I don't love her.'

'Did it ever look as if it would work?'

'She wanted to give me a child. After Bertie, she was insistent I should have, as she put it, one of my own. But afterwards we both knew things weren't knitting. She knew — women do, don't they — that my real self was engaged elsewhere and she just took off on her travels. In Brussels she met and fell in love with someone else.'

'I've heard about him. He's in politics too, isn't he?'

'Who told you?'

'I have an informant at the House.'

'Why won't you tell me who it is?'

'It's Brendan. Brendan Cassidy. He's hoping to make Parliament, too, you know. Meantime he's a researcher.'

'Do you see much of him?' he demanded jealously.

She did not answer the question directly. 'He's a good friend.'

'How good a friend? Are there others? There must be. You're an attractive woman.'

She savoured the small, sweet bonus of his jealousy. 'You have answered your own question.'

Somewhat moodily, he let in the gears of the big car. She took out her powder compact and lipstick and repaired the ravages of her tears. A heavy tension built up in her stomach at the thought of what lay ahead. They were moving into beautiful countryside, the countryside of rich farms and extravagant mansions, where money and privilege had sat comfortably over the centuries. She had to admit it was an England she scarcely knew. Deracinated London was one thing, she had been to Brighton and Manchester, but these lovely old Cotswold stones spoke another story, going far back into time.

When they came to the village adjoining Knoleberry

Park, Johnnie stopped in the main street and showed her the church and the memorial to the Cavaliers who had clashed with Cromwell's Roundheads. On a mossy old stone she deciphered the names of Reginald Dignam, his wife Henrietta and their sons, who had lived and breathed five centuries ago.

She began to know a little of what Johnnie was about, in the genetic and historic rather than the modern sense. Just as she knew, when she went back to the Western Isles of Scotland, that her own forebears had lived and breathed and had their being there, she knew now where Johnnie's roots lay and knowing that, owned the pull of his loyalties. It was all very different from her own background, golden and laconic and lush where hers was spare and misty and evanescent, but she saw you could love this place, belong to it in your secret necessary heart, as she belonged to Scotland and what it had laid on her bones.

They drove alongside a river lined with trees, past almshouses and thatched cottages that would drip in summer with roses and clematis and that were trimmed now with the fresh yellow and mauves of spring flowers, and as they turned a bend there were swans on the water and a vista of limpid, lovely fields, quiescent still because winter's quiet touch had not gone, not quite, and then stately and beautiful before its mass of dark firs, was Knoleberry.

Sixteen

Two little boys were playing on their tricycles in front of the house, watched by their nanny, a forbidding figure in her navy uniform.

When Helen and Johnnie got out of the car the children dismounted and came over to greet their father with kisses.

'This is a friend of mine, Miss Helen Maclaren,' said Johnnie. The children shook hands. Helen saw the younger had a front tooth missing. He was dark, smiling and irresistible. The older child, brown haired and already showing signs of sprouting into a lanky frame, was more wary. He hung on to Johnnie's hand, tugging it constantly for attention.

'Will you take us fishing, Papa?'

'I want to buy sweets.'

Johnnie looked at their navy-clad protector.

'Perhaps Nannie Walker will take you to the village?' he proposed, fishing in his pocket and coming up with sixpence each. Nannie Walker gave him a somewhat sour look but the children showed great enthusiasm for their father's notion. Mounting their tricycles they were off up the drive, shouting to each other how they were going to spend their pocket-money. To Helen they seemed happy, secure little boys. As why wouldn't they be, living in such ideal surroundings, well fed, well cared for at least in the practical sense? Memories of her own skinflint upbringing were uppermost as she took the mellow brown steps up to the front doors of Knoleberry.

Johnnie engaged her look, with a smile that was intended to reassure. They marched across a broad, flagstoned hallway, lined with armour, shields, swords, hung with dark oils. Johnnie pushed open double doors, a servant dodged through carrying a tray and then they were in a huge drawing-room, with a fire smoking in a cavernous, antler-hung fireplace, two black dogs stirring and wagging their tails amiably and the figure of Sir Bertram Dignam lighting a meerschaum pipe in the depths of a huge leather luggie chair. The old man struggled to his feet, giving Helen a curt bow of acknowledgement before collapsing again and resuming the struggle with his pipe.

'Father,' said Johnnie, 'I've brought Helen to see you,' – he brought Helen forward by the hand – 'to settle this matter of the editorship.' He tugged at the bell-pull. 'And we both need some coffee. What about you?'

'Had mine.' The handsome brows frowned at Helen. 'Matter's been settled, young woman. Board's decided you're too young. Too few qualifications. Handsome cash settlement, of course –'

'It's the second time you've offered me money.' Suddenly Helen was no longer unsure or tremulous. She sat down in one of the enormous chintz-covered chairs as though she had every right to do so and crossed her legs with a deliberate self-possession. 'You ought to know by now I can't be bought.'

The old man puffed on his pipe with a look that was almost a smirk of satisfaction at the confrontation. Then he said slowly and deliberately, as though he had given the matter great consideration, 'War, of course, changed women's position somewhat. Got a bit above themselves. War's over, though.'

Johnnie broke in angrily, 'This has nothing to do with the war or women's status, Father. It has to do with the important principle of editorial freedom. You know you are not playing fair. But there's something else you should know. Helen is going to be my wife when the divorce comes through.'

'Don't personally approve of divorce. Never divorced your mother though she ran off,' rumbled the old man. He sat up attentively and pointed his pipe at Helen. 'You thought how it might affect his political standing? Lot of people like their politicians squeaky clean, y'know. And this chap has a lot going for him. Why don't you clear off and leave him alone?'

It was said in quite a mild way, but meant to be totally dismissive. A maid came in at this point, bearing the coffee on a silver tray, and mercifully giving Helen time to control the seething anger inside her. When the girl had gone, she said, adopting the same level tone he had, 'How dare you address me like that? I don't care if you are Johnnie's father.'

'People should stick to their class,' said the old man, almost affable now. 'Said it plenty of times to the boy. Can't water down me convictions this stage.'

'Why shouldn't you? What's life about if it's not about learning? Took the war to teach you about the false dawn of Fascism, didn't it?'

He was suddenly no longer the genial old codger doing a bit of gentle baiting, but upright in his chair glaring at her ferociously.

'Be careful, young woman,' he advised in magisterial tones, 'what you say.'

'As you are careful? Why should only my susceptibilities be at risk? Look what you let your son in for, in your terrible arrogance. He will never forget what he saw in the death camps. I've got the strength to fight you now because I know there was something rotten and decadent in your pre-war attitude and that there is something rotten and selfish and self-seeking even now.'

'I served my country, as did my son.'

'You served your class. Johnnie is different. He knows who made the biggest sacrifices in both world wars. Like the Scottish regiments and the working-class lads from Lancashire and Yorkshire and the rest.'

'Where did you find this vixen?' The old man turned with his eyes popping to his son. 'Do you seriously propose she continues to edit the magazine of which I am chairman?'

Johnnie had been listening to the exchange between his father and Helen like a drowning man unsure for which shore to make. Now he said, with a cutting directness, 'Then resign. Resign your chairmanship. That's all you can do. As I came here to tell you, Helen stays.'

He rose, no longer able to contain himself. 'Come on, Helen. I'll take you round the grounds.' As they left the room, he turned and said curtly to his father, 'We'll be staying for lunch.'

'Then you'd better know. Your wife is coming to see the boys.' Johnnie took the news impassively, saying nothing.

As he and Helen began their walk, he said, 'Do you mind? About Simonette coming?'

'I'd rather not meet her.'

'It can't be avoided.'

'Then I'll meet her.' She walked with her head down, not seeing the old trees and the splendid views to the river. 'Johnnie, maybe I *should* go. Maybe I should resign.'

'Never.'

'I made Hugh Latimer certain promises, you see. If I can't do that –'

'He knew how hard it would be for you. It was a lot to ask. But he knew what you were made of.'

'I can't stand up to the whole board and Kenneth Fellowes. Already Fellowes has brought a stronger political element –'

'Then you do what you can.' He stopped in his stride, grasping her arms. 'I'm getting through to the old man. He'll huff and he'll puff but he'll back down.'

'Why should he?' she asked in genuine puzzlement.

'Because he knows he'll lose me if he doesn't,' he said grimly.

'I don't know.' They were climbing a steep incline towards a gazebo and she said, a little breathlessly, 'Life keeps getting more complicated. I just want to write and edit. Do my work.'

'Did you think you could do it in an ivory tower?' he asked, but gently. 'Because you can't you know. You have to fight your battles in the real world.'

The table in the dining-hall was huge and Sir Bertram took his place at the head of it, with Simonette and the boys placed on his right and Helen and Johnnie to the left. There was clear soup, fresh salmon, new potatoes in a chive dressing, but nobody ate with much relish or enjoyment. Jamie had traces of liquorice at the side of his mouth and had lost his appetite entirely.

Without looking once in Helen's direction, the old man led the talk down inconsequential byways and it was mainly Simonette and the little boys who joined in. Helen was glad of the chance to scrutinise Johnnie's wife. Close to, she was prettier than she had appeared at the Savoy, but there was an element of stress in her demeanour that showed she, too, was finding the luncheon something of an ordeal.

Helen noticed with a jealous little stab that her voice and expression softened when she spoke to Johnnie, her manner gentle and conciliatory. Her eyelids flicked only occasionally in Helen's direction. Almost as though she is shutting me out, thought Helen. The whole occasion was becoming more and more surreal.

Nannie Walker took the children away to read and rest for an hour after lunch. The adults moved into the conservatory for coffee and Simonette took the chair next to Johnnie, talking to him in a low, urgent voice that shut out the other two. Helen made no effort to converse with the old man, whose eyes began to shut despite a second cup of strong coffee. She gazed instead at yet another magnificent view. It occurred to her, for the first time in any serious sense, that if she and Johnnie did eventually marry, she would one day be mistress of all this. Perhaps Johnnie's love of his home would rub off on her. But nothing spoke to her as of now. In fact, it was as though the place resisted her, found her foreign. She was filled with a thin, querulous disquiet that contained at its heart the unavoidable assertion: she *was* out of place here. The old man was right. All that connected her with Knoleberry Park was her love for Johnnie. Would that be enough to make her a success as his wife?

She became aware of the old man's lizard gaze on her, almost as though he read her thoughts. As he stirred and indicated by various rumbling noises that he had had enough of Johnnie's *tête-à-tête* with Simonette, the two in the corner stirred and Johnnie rose, indicating that Helen should take his seat instead near Simonette.

He took his father by the arm and led the old man from the conservatory.

'I want you to myself.' Helen looked into the dark, anxious eyes opposite as Simonette leaned towards her in the same confidential way she had used towards Johnnie.

Helen managed a tense smile. 'Why is that?'

'People think,' said Simonette, 'that when you let a marriage go, you do so without regrets. I regret so much. Mostly the lack of security for my children. That's what Johnnie and I have been discussing. I want him to agree to let me have them. Otherwise I'll fight the divorce.'

'What does he say?'

'He wants them. But I think he wants you more. He wants the divorce going through smoothly and quickly. Can't get rid of me fast enough.'

'I don't think that's true. Can't you compromise over the children?'

'I don't think so,' said Simonette, stiffly. 'Elsom, who will be my new husband, wants them to come with me. He has to think of his public image. The boys will go away to school soon, anyhow, so it's all rather academic.'

'What do the children think?'

Simonette looked genuinely surprised. 'Who knows? They have to have their future decided for them, don't they? And they need a mother's nurturing.' She gave Helen a suddenly knowing, weary, acknowledging look. 'I know it may not appear like it. I've been away a lot. But I love my sons. Johnnie knows that.'

'So does he – love them.'

'He can see them in the holidays. Look, you do know about Johnnie's ambition? You do know what happens to M.P.s? Parliament swallows them whole. I won't want to go away from Elsom. My travels were because Johnnie and I made such a mess of things, but it's different this time. I know I'm not making a mistake. Even if I were a dilettante of a mother, the boys would still see more of me than of Johnnie. Doesn't that convince you?'

'It's up to you and Johnnie,' said Helen helplessly. 'I feel I am just a bystander.'

'Oh, Helen,' said Simonette, 'you have never been that.'

Helen did not know, for once, what to say. She stood feeling awkward and tongue-tied as a sixth-former.

'What is it between you and Johnnie?' The question burst out of Simonette and then she looked quickly away, as though wishing she had not said it.

Helen had a quick, hypnogogic image of herself and Johnnie, dancing, in the church hall the first time they met. It had all been said then. All of it laid out.

'I don't know,' she answered, honestly. 'It just is, that's all.'

'I can't hand them over, willy nilly.' Johnnie hit the driving-wheel with the edge of his hand, his face thunderous and strained. 'She cannot deny she has been with Elsom. She is the guilty party. I feel sure I would get custody of the boys.'

'Now you are the guilty party too.' Helen looked quickly at him. 'If such terms have any validity.'

'I won't see you,' he said, edgily, 'if it is going to affect the divorce. We have waited this long, we can wait a little longer.'

'You don't need to see me at all,' she said, on her mettle.

'Oh, darling, you know very well what I am saying. My boys are my responsibility.'

'Simonette feels the same.'

'She left them when they were babies. To do her travel book. I don't even want them to go away to school. I want a house they can come home to after school. A house in London, with you. I want to be there when they have problems. And when they haven't.'

'I have to agree with Simonette that when the House is sitting you will not have the time you want to spend with them. And what about going down to your constituency at Knoleberry Park?'

'We'd take the boys. They'd be part and parcel of all we

did.'

'I don't know, Johnnie. You're turning me into a mother. How do you know I'd make a good one?'

'I just know.'

She sighed. 'Well then, it *is* going to be a messy divorce then. Simonette's mind is made up.'

'We'll just have to keep in touch for a while by phone and letter. I'm not going to have you dragged in on this. That's one thing I'm decided on.'

She was silent, trying to recall in detail what the two little boys had looked like. Jamie's cow-lick. Bertie's long, spatulate hands. Their very clean knees, not like the grubby tennis-balls of knees of the boys she'd grown up with. Their hoarse, little boys' laughs. Could she get to know them, like them, *love* them? She refused to think at all about what Johnnie had just said. More separation? Her thoughts were raw, bleeding.

Johnnie broke in on them. 'About the other thing. Your job. I had a word with the old boy. He's still fizzing with annoyance over what he sees as your intransigence. But he's agreed not to hold up funds and that you should be given a little longer to get used to the new regime.'

'How did you get him to agree to that?'

'Reluctantly. By putting the words into his mouth.'

'It's never going to work.'

'You can make it. If he gives a little, you can give a little. It's known as compromise.'

'It isn't in my nature.'

'Then we're in for a bumpy ride.'

Seventeen

Although they had agreed on discretion, he came to see her sometimes.

She would not have been her mother's daughter had not the whole idea of Johnnie's divorce gnawed at her conscience. Where she had grown up marriage was for life, even if that marriage was a perpetual battleground. But if you took away the bits of paper and the ceremonial and looked at the relationship between herself and Johnnie in its essentials, she had always been the wife of his heart. It was Simonette who had been the intruder. At least, so it seemed to her.

It came back to the children. She spent the whole of one evening trying to put the case to Johnnie that he and Simonette should give their marriage one last chance because of Bertie and Jamie. Even if he had been willing, Johnnie said, which he was not, Simonette was determined to marry Elsom.

Her conscience would never be completely saved, but she decided that if Johnnie won custody of the children she would be as good a mother as she knew how. It was no good wishing for things to be perfect. And indeed, with Johnnie back in her life she was rediscovering a new strength and robust happiness, that could meet doubts and insecurities and overcome them.

She realised that the idealistic boy she had met and fallen in love with had lived through his war trauma and become a resolute and hard-working politician. The charismatic good looks won him ready listeners, but what he said was always touched by down-to-earth common sense and humanity.

Maybe people responded also to the element of the vulnerable in him, the part that seemed to say: I know what it's like. Some of the Tory papers tipped him for office – not yet, perhaps, but in the near future.

She tried to imagine how the little boys would feel if and when they were incorporated into their lives. She thought she would take them swimming – she was good at that, there had been public baths near the tenement in Glasgow. She would get Johnnie to take them on holiday to Scotland, show them the silver sands at Moray and take them fishing off Brodick Pier. She would find them good books to read, acquaint them with the dinosaurs at the Natural History Museum and the Impressionists at the Tate. She began to feel quite proprietorial towards them. It was not at all hard to love what Johnnie loved. In fact, it would be impossible to do otherwise.

In the office, Kenneth Fellowes was fighting her daily to take the magazine in the direction he and Sir Bertram wanted. She relented to the extent of allowing him to start a column called Political Diary, hoping to contain him. Perhaps that was what real maturity was about, she reflected: taking on the world as it was. She thought perhaps you had to cash in some of your dreams of moral perfection, you had to put a gloss on your insecurities. You had above all to be courageous and make sure courage did not become ruthlessness. But all this new maturity was because of Johnnie. Having someone who loved you and put you first added a whole new dimension to living.

It was in the tailpiece of Kenneth Fellowes' Political Diary that she learned of Brendan Cassidy standing as a

Parliamentary candidate. The old Labour warhorse had died and now, Fellowes predicted, there would be a ding-dong battle between a young Tory already well known as a television presenter and this 'dour Glaswegian' whom Labour had chosen.

It was the 'dour Glaswegian' that did it. At least, so she told herself, smiling. London hacks almost immediately prefixed any Scots name with 'dour'. She had a free Sunday and would not be seeing Johnnie so decided to visit Brendan in his constituency.

Johnnie had prevailed upon her to buy a small car and she drove past the busy Sunday markets in the East End towards Brendan's flat, wondering at the strength of the impulse taking her there. Certainly she wanted to wish him well, tell him she was glad he'd made it as candidate, 'dour' or not, ask him about Rose, whom she'd not seen for ages. And she wanted to share something with him. Wanted him to see she was happy. That this was a mixed motive was something she recognised. Whatever, the impulse to connect up with Brendan was so strong as to be irresistible. Her friend. Her *dear* friend. Maybe it was also about reiterating where she came from, about remembering her roots.

A dark, intense-looking young Jewish woman opened the door to Brendan's flat, revealing a scene of hive-live activity. Two older women and a small, shrunken man in a short-sleeved pullover were frantically folding election leaflets, while Brendan was talking urgently into the telephone.

'I'm an old friend of Brendan's,' said Helen, to the woman who had let her in. 'Gita Cohen,' said the woman, briefly. 'Find a seat if you can. Maybe you could make us all a cup of tea.'

Brendan waved in Helen's direction. His dark hair was standing up on end and his face was animated. Caught up in the atmosphere of desperate urgency,

Helen moved in an almost dream-like state towards the kitchenette and the kettle.

She was getting some message from the handsome, rather fierce person who had admitted her. Like a little animal, Gita Cohen seemed to be giving off a sense of territorial warning. Every line of her neat if thick-set little body seemed to be saying: this is my domain. I look after this man, I run this operation.

Helen relaxed a little as the water ran into the kettle. So maybe Brendan had met his match! Gita Cohen had fine dark eyes that sparkled with a sharp intelligence. Had she recognised in Brendan another *mensch*, someone of heart and dignity who only needed a total affection from someone to grow to full stature? The part of Helen that was truly attached to Brendan, that cared for him and wanted things to work out for him, won out over the greedy, smaller, female part that had thought *she* would always be special. But she was only speculating. Perhaps her intuition was wrong. As she set out the mugs and put tea in the big aluminium teapot she realised that something more than impulse might have brought her here. Maybe the unconscious need for Brendan was for her to close a chapter.

She heard the telephone receiver go down and waited for Brendan to come to her in the kitchen. He did, with a broad, shy smile on his face. He did what he was normally too inhibited to do on greeting her; he kissed her.

'What brings you here, old chum, old friend?'

'I hadn't heard from you. Then I read you were standing for Parliament. Will you get in?' His kiss was still burning her mouth, her hand feeling pins and needles from his hard shake. In the room beyond she could see Gita's broad listening back.

'Well, you know what we're up against. Lady voters kiss my opponent goodnight on the telly. He's as much part of their lives as hot cocoa.'

It was all too much for Gita. She advanced through the open door, making no pretence of not having listened to every word. Putting her arms about Brendan's shoulders she said, 'People know this is a good man. He's worked in the constituency for years when there was no advantage in it for him. He's been the best councillor we've had and now he's going to be the best candidate.' She held Brendan's arm possessively and kissed him, not once but twice.

Brendan's arm snaked round Gita's waist, squeezing it. 'Look at the support I've got!' he boasted. He smiled down at Gita. 'You know who Helen is? She's my old Glasgow chum. We used to go to night school together.'

Gita gazed at Helen with a certain open challenge. Not smiling. 'I may have heard of her,' she said, a trace of her German-Jewish origins in her accent. 'I do not quite remember.'

Helen put the mugs on a tray. 'Let's take these through to the others,' she suggested. The leaflet workers scarcely paused in their labours to thank her. Brendan followed her. 'Do you remember the blackout?' he was saying. 'And the arguments we used to have about practically everything? This girl,' he addressed his audience, 'has an encyclopaedic mind and an answer to everything.'

Helen mugged it up. 'And I'm beautiful with it,' she laughed.

'You are too thin, perhaps,' suggested Gita.

Brendan's gaze lighted on Helen. It said: don't pay any attention. This is how it is. But I think I might love her. I think I may be over my long obsession with you.

She said directly to Gita, 'I can't stay. I am holding you all up,' and saw the anxiety fade from the girl's eyes to be replaced by a placatory warmth. 'Fold some leaflets,' Gita instructed. 'You do not need to leave yet, surely.'

In the midst of the afternoon's activities, with the
telephone ringing and the doorbell going incessantly,
Helen managed to ask Brendan about Rose. 'I phoned
her several times, but she blames me for Frankie taking
Sean away. She won't talk to me.'

'I don't see much of her,' he admitted. 'She is dancing
for a living. What do they call them? Show-girls? He is
not averse to having her dance.' He spread his hand in a
gesture of helplessness.

'Not in the revue bars?'

'Whatever. Last time I saw her, she was talking of
going legit, as she called it. Getting into a stage musical.
We don't seem to connect either since Sean went. She
seems harder, somehow.'

'Not hard.' Helen shook her head. 'Probably just
getting by as best she can, Brendan. Look,' she
promised, 'I'll try to see her again. I'll *make* her see me.
We can't lose touch.'

'It'll be a waste of time.' He gave her an apologetic
look. 'She's cut all her links with the past, it seems. And
that's that.'

It was strange, sitting there in the big shabby room
filled with its sense of battling expectancy. Helen saw
how Brendan's life had been leading up to this and how
now he was tuned for the fight, like a young gladiator.

Different from Johnnie. She had not been there when
Johnnie fought his Parliamentary battle, but she knew it
would have been on an altogether different plane. Not
less worthy, perhaps. But he had fought from a position
of privilege, the seat he took a safe one. While Brendan
had had to engage in a long slow war of attrition,
fighting first his own and then others' ignorance. A
lonely, shabby man with grubby shirt cuffs. She might
love Johnnie, but this man touched her spirit because
they had both come up from the same scrappy
beginnings.

Brendan eased up beside her on the settee. One of the older women had declared she was off to make her family's tea and Gita was at the door, seeing her off.

'You seem – different,' said Brendan. 'What is it?'

'I'm going to marry him after all. Johnnie.'

'Is he divorced, then?'

'No, but he soon will be.'

'Should you give him another chance?'

'I don't seem to have much option. I love him.'

'I know that.' He looked at her, with the same old depth of feeling she had always known was in him, with the same old jealous anger. 'That's not what I'm asking.'

'Does he love me?' She put the question for him and he looked quickly away from the radiance on her face. 'Yes. yes, he does.'

'I might marry Gita,' he said, cautiously. She nodded in quiet acknowledgement. 'I think it might work,' she said. She didn't know what else to say. Suddenly it seemed possible to talk to Brendan more openly than she had ever done before, but she could not, with all these people around them. Suddenly she wanted to tie up the loose ends of their relationship but it refused to happen. There was an ache somewhere in her as there was, in him. She could tell from his troubled expression. Gita came back into the room and the moment passed. Quite soon Helen rose and looked for her coat.

Brendan came into the tiny lobby to see her off. They were in such confined space it was easy to embrace her. 'Helen,' he said and she knew some things were never over, some feelings would never fade. He kissed her on her mouth, as he had done when she arrived. It was a breaking off, a relinquishment, and why had she thought it would be painless?

'I won't run this,' said Helen angrily. She threw the copy down on Kenneth Fellowes' desk.

He looked up almost sunnily. 'Why not? A by-election in the East End. A topic of some interest, I would have thought.'

'You know it's not mention of the by-election I object to. It's the four pars in praise of Robin Broadstock and the one snide mention of the Labour man. He's not a "Glasgow hard man" and he's not a "Clyde red".'

'Come on, we all use political shorthand.'

'Broadstock's getting enough coverage on telly as it is.'

It was his turn to go prickly. 'Look,' he said heatedly, 'what I've written is fair comment. Broadstock's got the superior education, he's travelled the world. Cassidy's still rough round the edges –'

'I know Cassidy. No way is he the hick you present in this.'

'Look, my mandate from the board and chairman is clear. I am the *Spectrum*'s political man and I write what I like, without fear or favour.'

'And I exercise my editorial discretion about fair play.' Helen walked angrily back towards her cubby-hole, calling back over her shoulder, 'At least go down to the Cassidy camp and find out what he's on about.'

She could hear Fellowes' angry muttering that he would do no such thing. Their battles were becoming almost daily and she knew where Fellowes was getting the back-up to challenge her. She looked back on the days when the gentle, unobtrusive Hugh had wrested some of the best writing in London from his small band of contributors, as always making that which was difficult appear easy because of his unerring taste and judgement. She wouldn't, she couldn't give up the standards he had set, even she didn't always reach them.

But Fellowes rattled her, and knew that he did. It was part of the unacknowledged game by which she would be forced out and he would take over. She thought of Johnnie's father and could see no option but another row with him. To think the hard-bitten old scoundrel would one day be her father-in-law!

The telephone rang on her desk and Johnnie's voice said in her ear, 'How's my best girl?' He sounded happy and excited and she ironed the irascibility from her own voice as she answered, 'I'm in the pink. What's up?'

'I'm going on a Parliamentary delegation to the Middle East – Israel, Jordan, all that. What I've always wanted. Harris has dropped out due to illness. Just wish you could come.'

'Be careful.' The words were out before she had time to censor them. She did not want him going anywhere. Not yet. Till the day they went everywhere together. 'Johnnie, hasn't there been fighting in Jordan? People killed in the villages?'

'Yes.' He laughed reassuringly. 'But we'll be looked after. It's in everybody's interest to get peace in the Middle East. To give Israel a chance.'

'When are you going?'

'Tomorrow. First thing. Doesn't look as though I'll see you first. So be good. And just one thing –'

'Yes. What?'

'I love you. Don't forget.'

'I love you. And take care.'

There was one thing to be said in the phone call's favour. It put all thoughts of Kenneth Fellowes and his mean-spirited assaults on her territory out of her mind.

She was glad for Johnnie, of course, glad to hear him so happy and confident. Foreign affairs were something he wanted to be more and more involved in and he saw a stable State of Israel as being the one way the world could compensate for what had happened to the Jews in the death camps.

And of course they would be well looked after. It wasn't in any government's interest to allow any parliamentary delegation to stray where there might be danger. But the Middle East was to say the least unpredictable and British-Israeli relations still tinged with bitterness from past conflicts. If this was what loving somebody did to you, she thought wryly, tying you in emotional knots the minute they're out of your ken, then it's a poor do. She would keep busy – there was plenty to do, at home and at work. And soon Johnnie would be back home again.

But when she saw a plane soar eastwards as she walked towards the tube the next morning, she thought prayerfully of all travellers and particularly of the one precious to her called Johnnie Dignam.

Eighteen

'Is that Helen Maclaren?'

She knew who the caller was immediately, of course, even if the harsh buzz of the telephone had dragged her out of the sweet depths of early morning sleep. She knew, too, that it could not be good news to be conveyed at this hour, six-thirty, or by the caller, Johnnie's father, Sir Bertram Dignam. Totally alert, not feeling the chill of the unheated room on her bare shoulders, she demanded, 'What is it?'

'I wanted you to know before the papers reach you or the reporters get to your door.' The voice was curiously ironed of emotion, curiously neutral. 'My son and another M.P., the Labour man, Colin Fowkes, have gone missing from the delegation.'

'Gone missing?' Despite her alertness, she could not make sense of this. 'How could they go missing? Don't they know where they've gone? Have they been – taken, kidnapped, or something?' She was babbling, the hand she used to run the last of sleep from her face suddenly damp with perspiration. She sat up in a kneeling position, suddenly able to see a milk-float, a milkman with his load of early bottles, through the fine net of her windows. If normal procedures were taking place, down there in the street, why was it so difficult to make sense of what was going on in her head?

'Helen.' The calm, deliberate voice again. 'I want you

to keep your wits about you today. Say nothing to anyone. Perhaps it would be as well if you stayed away from the office.'

'I have to go in. It's publication day.'

'Then I'll try to get in to see you. We'll have to play this very carefully. If he is being held – and we don't know that – any speculation will simply be useful to their captors.'

'Nothing can happen to him.' She did not know whether this was a useless reassurance to herself or a plea for reassurance from this man she so disliked.

'He will be all right.' The voice, unexpectedly kindly, brought tears of shock. 'Look, it isn't wise to say any more at the moment. I will keep you informed.'

She got up and dressed in a kind of daze, realising when she had all her clothes on that she had neither washed nor brushed her teeth. She must have made tea, because she was drinking it from a cup that shook on the saucer.

Why was it only Fowkes and Johnnie were missing, out of a delegation of eight? Had they gone off on an exploration of their own or had they been lured by some mysterious invitation? There would be plenty in Israel who would have no love for the son of Sir Bertram Dignam, with the latter's well known prewar fraternisation with the likes of Ribbentrop. And what about the Arabs? Could they have seized the two Englishmen willy-nilly, as pawns in the complicated game that was Middle Eastern politics? Was it possible that Fowkes and Johnnie, spurred by the need to know what went on at ground level, had unwisely taken themselves off on private investigations and simply got lost? Unlikely. The cold realisation was coming to her that kidnapping was the likeliest of the scenarios and if that was the case there would doubtless be a ransom.

When she got to the office, she saw immediately that

Kenneth Fellowes knew. 'It's possible that the pair of them took off into the desert and got lost, you know,' he said. 'They could have run out of petrol. Anything.'

'Why would they do that?' she demanded, dully.

'I dunno. Just that sometimes the unlikeliest explanation for something is the right one. Look here, I can run the show if you want to go home.'

'I'm better here.' She gave him a quick smile of gratitude. She sent Kimberley out for the earliest editions of the evening paper, on the streets before lunchtime. The *Standard* said M.P.s HELD TO RANSOM? and the *Evening News* MYSTERY OF MISSING M.P.s but apart from hinting there was a flurry of Foreign Office activity the stories shed no light on what might really have happened.

Kimberley brought in some sandwiches and dealt with phone calls from Fleet Street, most of whom knew about Helen's association with Johnnie Dignam. In the afternoon, the old man came into the office, with two men who could have been Special Branch. Sir Bertram squeezed himself into the only chair, apart from the editorial one, in Helen's office, spreading his hands in a gesture of helplessness. 'We can only wait,' he said. His normally florid complexion looked curiously drained. 'Think,' he said to Helen. 'Was there anything he said to you before he went that might give us a lead? Anything?'

'Only that he wanted to make it exhaustive. That there was so much to find out.'

'His curiosity might have landed him in this predicament. He may have been persuaded to talk to some outlandish faction –'

'And not realised the dangers.' They were talking the same language now, the language of terror. She noticed how the old man's hand had a fine tremor as it lay on her desk.

'The Foreign Office won't give in to blackmail. That's a road they won't go down.'

'But if it was simply money? What if it is simply that? Couldn't we raise whatever is asked?'

He looked at her and blinked, once. The thought entered her mind and lodged there that he knew more than he was telling her. He shook his head and fell silent.

'What about the boys?' she asked. 'Do they know?'

'Fortunately they are with their mother. In France. On holiday. She will tell them only what she thinks they ought to know.'

She had some straightforward work to do after Sir Bertram's visit. Although the magazine had gone to press, she had to prepare early pages for the new edition and the discipline of work gave her a measure of composure. She kept thinking there would be some news soon. British citizens, especially British parliamentarians, could not just disappear off the face of the earth. Kenneth Fellowes did his best to commiserate and encourage. At five o'clock she went home and switched on her recently acquired television set. She had a sensation of sinking into the mire of nightmare. What if they were never found? What if, when found, they ...? Her mind went round and round in tortuous speculation.

Each time the telephone rang she answered, in case there should be news, but she kept commiserative talk to a minimum, hunching back in her chair and watching the television screen with a strange, blank concentration.

At six o'clock the doorbell rang and she answered it, determined to send any cursory caller away. It was Rose Cassidy who stood there. She wore a familiar shabby full-skirted grey coat and a navy hat with a fraction of veiling and she smiled nervously. 'Can I come in?' she said.

Helen opened the door wider. 'What wind blew you?' she demanded drily.

'When your mother was in trouble, she went to my mother. And vice-versa,' said Rose quickly. 'Remember?' Both hands held her handbag handle. 'I can always make a cup of tea,' she offered.

Helen's arms opened to embrace her friend. Suddenly, apart from her own mother, Rose was the only person she wanted in the same room. Rose's hands patted her back. 'Come on,' she said gently. 'I came as soon as I heard the news. Brendan told me – about you and Johnnie Dignam. I should have been in touch sooner.'

'What will I do, Rose, if anything's happened to him?'

Rose did not answer. Calmly she put away her coat and hat, entered the kitchen, laid a tray, boiled the kettle, made toast. Helen watched her, half transported back to that crowded kitchen, with a big coal fire on the range, that had been the Cassidy home in Glasgow. A place where, for all its shortcomings, there had always been human warmth and reaching out. She didn't want to lose that feeling of humanity, ever. It was here now, with Rose.

Rose handed her a cup of tea. It was sweet and she no longer took sugar, but she drank gratefully, tasting and enjoying it as she hadn't tasted anything all day.

Rose said, 'I wouldn't have taken a bet on you and Johnnie ever getting together again. What happened? Do you want to tell me about it?'

In the old days, the Glasgow days, they had sat on tussocky grass in the park and talked about the boys they liked in their respective school classes and later, at the little tables on the edge of dance floors, exchanged confidences and blushes. When Rose had been teased and assaulted by older children, Helen had come to the rescue and once, when Helen had dirtied a clean frock by missing a puddle jump, Rose had nobly insisted it was half her fault and deflected the hard edge of Mrs

Maclaren's hand from her friend. Together, they'd made sugarolly water from liquorice straps, played peever and counted each other in on complicated skipping-rope rituals, wiped grimy tears from each other's faces and dashed off bright-faced to the Saturday matinées of Laurel and Hardy at the pictures.

Once again it was that easy, the comradeship between them. Easy to tell Rose of her misgivings, of how seeing Johnnie again had produced the same irrefutable feelings. Easy to weep and laugh and confess. And forget, for a moment, the terror.

'I don't think you've changed at all, underneath,' said Rose. 'I don't think we do. We are the children we used to be, only bigger. You always knew exactly what you wanted, Helen. You were always determined. You dress nicely now and have your hair done, but all I can see is the Helen who wouldn't go to a party because the hem had been let down on her dress and the mark showed.'

'I don't remember …'

'You were about eight. Seven, maybe. You went eventually in your ordinary school skirt and jumper. The dress had belonged to a cousin or something. Anyhow, you didn't feel it was right for you and nothing, no power on earth, would make you wear it. I can still see your mother's face, a mixture of fury and annoyance and yet she knew you had your own standards and she could only respect them.'

'Fancy you remembering that!'

'Johnnie's a bit like that. I mean, he's the one you want and that's it. Other people fall in and out of love. Not you.'

'You mean most people can love more than one person? I think you're right.' Helen looked curiously at her friend. 'You can, can't you?'

'If you mean, did I love Frankie, yes I did. And if you mean do I love Guido, the answer's yes, too. Not in the same way —'

'What way, then? Tell me. I'd really like to know.'

'In an older way. A wiser way. I don't expect him to be perfect. Just as well, because perfect he ain't.'

'Brendan thinks he exploits you.'

'What does Brendan know about love? Apart from the useless torch he's always carried for you —'

'He knows now. I've been to see him and there's something going on between him and a Jewish girl, called Gita.'

Rose was stopped in her tracks. 'You think he'll marry her?'

'I think if he wins this by-election, he will. He'll need someone like her, she's an organiser, an able, committed lady.'

'Why doesn't he come to see me?'

'Because you didn't want to see either of us for a while, did you?' Helen chose her words with care. 'I want you to know I'm sorry, Rose. For interfering over Sean. The last thing I wanted was to hurt you —'

'You did right.' Rose's words were clipped but her voice held traces of the hurt she denied. 'I'm easier in my mind now about Sean. He writes to me, they send me photographs of him. He seems to have broadened out, become an all-American boy. Maybe he likes the all-male situation over there. And his grandmother spoils him.'

Helen looked away. The Rose she was seeing was once again the deprived little waif of the tenement stairs, heir to perpetual hand-me-downs that didn't fit. The kid her mother Jessie always managed to find an extra slice of bread and jam for, the one always with a younger child by the hand or in her arms. She felt a rush of tenderness and protest, an overwhelming wish that life should work out for Rose, bring her some of the rewards she deserved. She had always known that Rose was in some ways a superior human being to herself – less self-absorbed, less selfish, less prideful. It had been an act of savagery to take her child away. Yet there had been no option. Guido was the enigma in Rose's life, with his dark, macho temper that had made life so miserable for Sean.

As if she were reading her mind, Rose said now, 'You wouldn't understand, Helen, but Guido needs me, even more than Sean does.'

Helen shook her head in mystification.

'He gambles. It's easy to criticise but it's the atmosphere he's been brought up in. Italian women put their men on pedestals. They can do no wrong. They get to be wilful and greedy. Yet he tries not to be. In his own way, he tries to look after me –'

'He lets you dance in these sleazy places.' Helen could not forbear interrupting.

'But nothing happens to me!' Rose looked at Helen the way an elderly aunt might look at an amusing child.

'But something might!'

'I like to dance. I'm taking proper lessons. Everybody has to begin somewhere.' Rose got up. She was not as composed as her words indicated. 'See, I live in the world as it is, Helen. You and the likes of Brendan, you think what you do will change things, but it won't, in the end, human nature being what it is.'

'What awful pessimism!' Helen joked.

'It isn't! If you start off with my view, you don't get let down. You might even get a few nice surprises along the way. When Guido wins on the horses, he'll go out and buy me a gold cross, or a big fancy box of chocs. And he'll sweep the stairs to the flat when I'm tired.'

The waif on the stairs. With the big, tragic eyes. *We're the children we used to be, only bigger.*

It was beginning to get dark outside. A clear night, with the North Star brightly visible. Helen stepped outside the magic circle of the past and back into the present. She turned the sound up again on the television, then down as a game show came on.

The telephone shrilled and she pounced on it. Rose saw her face go pinched and withholding. 'I'll be all right,' she said into the receiver. 'I have an old friend from Glasgow with me. Yes, ring me if there is anything.'

'Who was it?'

Helen sat down and played with the signet ring that Johnnie had bought her all those years ago, in Glasgow.

'His father. Johnnie's father. At least he talks to me. It takes this to make him talk to me.' Her face broke up and she held a hand over her eyes. She waited for some composure to return then said, 'Rose, what shall I do if I never see him again?'

'Don't be so daft! Of course you'll see him.'

'There was something in the old man's voice. I think maybe he knows more than I do. He's – he's frightened, Rose. And so am I.'

Rose clicked out the main light, leaving only a soft glow from a table lamp. She sat down on the chair opposite Helen.

'There was this priest. He came to me after Sean went away. And he said to me, "Life is a flame. You have to tend it till it goes out." You have to keep the flame going, no matter how poor a wee flame it gets to be and one day, it lights up everything. What he said was true, Helen. I'm here to tell you.'

She wanted to argue against Rose's homespun philosophy but something tied her tongue. She grasped at the comfort offered. It wasn't the words themselves: it was the impulse of pure human kindness behind them that she needed.

Nineteen

The newspapers brought out their boldest type over the next two days and entertained every kind of speculation, no matter how wild, how gloomy.

Helen talked her way into the press briefings at the Foreign Office and it was there on the third day that the first glimmering of genuine news broke through.

Harvey Bentley, the press officer, young and keen with a silly-ass laugh, a Cambridge education and a sharp mind, dashed into the midst of loitering journalists bearing a message aloft like a flag.

'It seems,' he announced, 'that a small group of Israeli fanatics have taken Dignam and Fowkes. Nothing to do with the Israeli Government, who are aghast at the whole affair. Everything to do with some near-private vendetta – the leader of the faction once belonged to the Stern Gang and may be paying off an old score.'

He lowered the hand bearing the message, his moment of high drama over. 'The rest we have to wait for,' he advised his audience. 'Of course the Government is doing everything in its power to obtain the release of these British citizens. It is unthinkable that anything should happen to them –'

'How are they?' shouted the *Express* man.

'We don't know.'

'But they're alive?'

'So far as we know.' Bentley did not bat an eyelid.

'You must have more news.' Helen pressed her way through her colleagues. Her teeth seemed to be sticking to her dry lips, her legs felt like mechanical legs. 'You must know if they are safe.'

'Miss Maclaren.' Bentley recognised his interrogator, as everyone else did in the room. There were murmurs of sympathy and support. 'We are doing all we can. You will get any further news the moment we clear it.'

'Helen.' It was Sydney Felder, her tormentor from the days when Hugh Latimer had been editor, but prepared now to forget the inferior status of women on the scent of the best story of the day. His sharp, perceptive gaze traversed her face. 'How bad's it been? Are you and Johnnie's father at one in this? How do you get on with the old tyrant these days?'

'How can you?' she spat at him. 'Making copy out of people's agony.'

He took her elbow, almost companionably. 'Listen,' he said, keeping his voice as low as possible, 'I've heard they want the old man out there. To make him eat humble pie.'

'Where did you hear that?'

'Can't tell you. I've heard: no negotiations till Sir Bertram Dignam goes to the Middle East. Do you think he'll play ball, eh Helen? Do you know anything I don't know?'

She shook herself free. 'Why should they do that to an old man? His health is not good.' Felder looked at her in surprise. The conflict between her and Sir Bertram was common knowledge in Fleet Street. The veteran newsman gave a sardonic smile. 'The crisis makes strange bedfellows, eh?'

She wanted to remonstrate, to insist that she and Sir Bertram had nothing in common except the safety of Johnnie Dignam, but what did it matter? She had a feeling the situation was spinning too fast towards its

denouement and that if she did not keep a grip on
reality things would go out of control. It was irrational,
but that was how she felt.

Leaving the briefing, she pointed her car towards
Victoria, thinking to call at Sir Bertram's flat but then
changed her mind. It would be besieged by the usual
battery of reporters and photographers and if she went
there it would only complicate matters. Instead she went
back to the office. Kenneth Fellowes stood waiting for
her at the top of the stairs, having heard her footsteps.

'I've got news for you,' he said. 'Sir Bertram is flying
out to Israel.'

'I want to go with him.'

'He said you'd say that. He says it's important you stay
here. Anyhow, he's already on his way.'

She lost control a little then. 'Who makes decisions for
me?' she shouted at Fellowes. 'I want to be where
Johnnie is. I want him to know I'm there.' She was
shaking and weeping and ashamed of both reactions.
Blindly she held out her hands towards Kimberley, who
led her into her office and brought the customary cup
of grey Kimberley tea.

Fellowes waited till the anxious girl had completed
her ministrations then deliberately closed the door on
Helen and himself.

'Come on,' he soothed, 'you've been marvellous up
till now. Just hang on a little longer.'

'Why do they want the old man? Do they want money
out of him? Some kind of recantation of his prewar
views? What does it matter now? Johnnie did all any
human being could to restore the family name.'

Fellowes looked at her strangely. 'It isn't quite as you
think it is.'

Helen's head came up with a look of fierce enquiry.
'How is it, then?'

'Different from what everyone thinks. I can't say any

more. I'm not in a position to say any more. But keep
your powder dry, Helen. Be brave for Johnnie.'

It was a new Kenneth Fellowes she saw. Or perhaps
not so new. She had maybe known that another, kinder
side existed apart from the almost helplessly ambitious
one. He could not be more considerate now, taking
phone calls, warding off callers, feeding her work that
could be coped with, with half her mind. It was all part
of the strange, surreal texture of that day, a day when
she was tortured by thoughts of Johnnie and Fowkes
being starved and ill treated, imprisoned in some dark,
airless hell-hole, not knowing if they would ever come
out alive.

She tried to pray but was frightened away from the
act by the terror and anger she felt towards her Maker:
she thought she should approach Him with more
humility yet it was not there. She tried sending out the
power of her thoughts towards Johnnie – useless, she
knew, but she did it anyway: darling, don't give up.
Think what lies ahead for us. Don't leave me now we
have just found each other again.

She imagined her love wrapped round him like a
cocoon, like a magic shawl.

Her thoughts also veered wildly in search of some
practical course of action. Should she fly out to Israel
too, despite the advice against it offered all round?
Would it make matters worse or better? Where would
she stay? Who could she see?

She was in a state of near exhaustion when she left the
office. Rose had promised to return that evening, to
make sure she had a proper meal, but not until eight.
Perhaps the decision as to how she would fill the next
two hours had been formulating all afternoon. For
Simonette had flitted in and out of her mind – how she
might be feeling, whether she too might be feeling cut
off and starved of information.

She just had the hunch that Simonette and the boys might have returned from France. The wealthy Elsom had made a flat available to her in Knightsbridge – Johnnie had pointed it out to her once – and it was just feasible she would be there. Once Helen had decided to explore the possibility, it seemed like the most positive thing for her to do. What Johnnie would want her to do. Strange, that.

The flat was somewhere behind Harrods and not all that easy to locate again. The door opened on a strong security chain and Simonette's face devoid of any make-up, peered warily round it.

'How did you know I was back?' She was not about to release the chain or give admittance.

'Just a hunch.' Helen leaned against the lintel. She felt, suddenly, deathly tired, unable to offer explanations. Simonette hesitated for a further moment and then somewhat ungraciously released the security chain and said, 'Come in.'

Helen followed her into a large, gracious room furnished mainly in silvery greys with crimson velvet cushions. One large chair bore the indentation of Simonette's body, with a table in front of it bearing wine in a bottle, a half-empty glass, and an ashtray with a number of lip-sticked stubs. Simonette emptied the stubs into a wastepaper basket. 'Sorry,' she offered. 'But it's been that kind of day.'

'The boys?'

'Elsom's taken them to his mother's. It's not good for them to see me – see me, well, distraught like this.'

'How are they taking it?'

'Well, they don't know everything. And they sense the undertow of mystery and want to find out more. It's a strain. Wine?'

'No thanks.'

'You know Sir Bertram has gone? To Israel?'

'Yes. And I'm a bit like the boys. I feel an undertow of mystery, as you put it. I don't know *why* and although I can't pretend he and I get on, I'm desperately worried for him.'

'Is that why you came here?'

'I suppose so. I mean, the old man's the last person to negotiate with Israelis of whatever complexion, never mind the fanatical sort.'

Simonette said nothing. Helen was aware of her rearranging her position on the big easy chair, of perhaps conducting some internal argument with herself.

'You and I are going to have to rub along together, for the sake of the children,' said Simonette at length. She lit another cigarette, took a deep inhalation and said, 'What I say to you now is in the strictest confidence. I don't know the various terms but the old man was a double agent.' Her voice lowered till Helen had to strain to hear it. 'All that prewar fratting with the enemy, it was a front, a bluff. One he's kept up till the present time because they are still chasing them, you know, some of the Nazi criminals. Sir Bertram has friends of the most enormous influence in the Middle East. If anyone can get Fowkes and Johnnie back, he can.'

It was so preposterous that Helen could not take it in at first. She thought: Simonette's had too much wine, this is fearful indiscretion, she should never have told me. But part of her was rejoicing, because if what she said was true, then Johnnie could be released. If anyone can get him back, Sir Bertram can, Simonette had said. Was it really true? Helen ran the conversation back on the sound-track of her mind. It had to be true. Simonette could not make up anything so outlandish.

'Simonette,' she said. 'Should you have told me this?'

'I suppose not.' Simonette waved the hand holding

the cigarette. 'But you're family. I'm going to trust you with my children so why shouldn't you be trusted with the family secrets? Johnnie trusts you utterly and he is not wrong about people.'

'Does Johnnie know? About his father?'

'I think he may. But if he does, he'll be sworn to the deepest secrecy. It was Elsom who told me. I dragged it out of him, one night in bed.'

'Fleet Street might get hold of it.' She was thinking of Sydney Felder. She was sure he did have the real story but his unfailing intuitive news sense, that ability that marked the first-class reporter from the merely good, had told him there was something there that hadn't yet been unfolded.

And Kenneth Fellowes. His gnomic '*It isn't quite as you think it is.*' He was very close to Sir Bertram and again his almost uncanny ability to suss out the secret, the unnameable, had perhaps put him at least partially in the picture.

Going over and over these preoccupations, it was as though Helen was trying to pick up something in Simonette's recent words that she had missed first time round.

I am going to trust you with my children. That was what she had said, wasn't it? She had been so caught up with the main theme she had not picked up the almost throwaway sentence. Now she started forward in her chair and demanded urgently, 'Simonette? What did you say about the children? Entrusting *me*, did you say?'

Simonette began to laugh, a high-pitched, nervous laugh that could be something of a release from all the unbearable strain. When she laughed, she was a good deal prettier and younger all of a sudden and Helen decided, as she had done before, that she and Simonette could at least get on the same wavelength, at least part of the time. She gave a reluctant smile and admitted, 'It has only just sunk in. What you said.'

'I'm going to make some sandwiches,' Simonette decided. She led the way into the kitchen. 'I don't think I've eaten all day. Cheese or pâté?'

'Cheese, I think,' said Helen, absently. 'No, pâté.'

'You see,' said Simonette, when she had taken a bit of some hastily spread bread, 'I'm in the throes of a balancing act. Elsom wants the divorce to go through quickly so we can get married. He doesn't want me to hold things up with quibbles about the children, though he'd like me to have custody. Typical, wants it both ways! And then, very important –' she flashed Helen a quick look – 'I've been asked to do another travel book. I expect you can understand better than anyone – I want a career of my own and I'm going to have to be a bit selfish. All in all, I think it's better if we revert to Plan A and I let Johnnie have the children. It'll be more stable. I do veer a bit, you see, from being earth-mother to being a proper writer. I think Elsom understands.'

She talks of Johnnie, Helen thought rebelliously, as if he will be restored to us. How can she know that? And yet part of her was grateful, played along. You had to think the best. The other was insupportable.

Helen spread the pâté on her piece of French bread with wobbly concentration. 'It can't be easy,' she offered. 'But yes, if you and I are friends, friends of a sort, it should make it easier for the boys.'

'They're very lovable,' said Simonette impulsively.

'I know.' They carried their sandwiches back into the sitting-room. 'I'm used to a lot of children,' said Helen. 'Working-class kids are. No nannies, you see. I was always looking after some neighbour's infant or other.' She thought of the children in the close – the Cassidy brood, her own brothers and sisters, the little cataract of children, in tackety boots, sandshoes or wellingtons descending from the flats above. She thought Bertie and

Jamie would be a doddle, compared to that.

'Shall we turn on the news?' demanded Simonette. Both pushed their plates away, not hungry any more.

'The Foreign Office has stepped up its demands for the release of the two parliamentarians, Mr John Dignam and Mr Colin Fowkes, being held prisoner in the Middle East.' The bland tones of the news-reader flowed over the pictures of desert, of soldiers, of fiery-looking men bearing guns. The kind of pictures taken from stock when there was nothing new to reveal. There was no mention of Sir Bertram's flight. The Foreign Office must have placed an embargo on the news.

Simonette looked at Helen's face and her hand came out quickly and grasped the other's. 'I wish there were something I could say that would make you feel better.'

'Three days,' said Helen. 'I never thought three days could be such a long time.'

Twenty

Rose had brought Helen some minestrone soup in a lidded can, made by her mother-in-law. 'Only the Scots and the Italians know how to make proper soup,' she had declared and stood over Helen while she supped it. She had gone to bed after listening to the late news on television and seeing Rose off in a taxi.

Helen was trying hard to cope with the new knowledge she had about Johnnie's father. What they called it back home was having the size of someone. She had always known she did not have the size of Sir Bertram. She had hated and disliked him and practically everything he stood for – his elitism, his snobbery, his harsh attitude towards everyone outside his class and especially towards her. Written about by the likes of P.G. Wodehouse, he could have appeared either funny or pathetic. Encountered by someone outside the magic circle he was rigid, cruel, unapproachable. The war had blown away many of the old class shibboleths but he stuck out like some rocky promontory on the landscape of the new classlessness. Even his Secret Service work, the fact of his having been a double agent, as Simonette alleged, was probably a way of shoring up what he regarded as his: land, privilege, status. England, his England. It was ridiculous how he brought out a fierce chauvinistic, egalitarian pride in her for her background, her heritage. The old ways were passing away, after all. He would soon be like the dinosaur, buried in the forgotten past.

It was the day of the common man. You could not ask a man to risk his all in a war then push him back into the same old mould, exploited and abused, overworked or unemployed. Somehow or other, men and women of goodwill had to find a fairer way and that surely meant an intermingling and then a dissolution of the classes. People like Johnnie had taken this philosophy on board without any trouble – she had noticed how he and his friends had even shelved their Oxford accents for something a lot less identifiable.

And yet ... She lay in bed thinking how brave the old man had been. To have had the guts to mix with the prewar German diplomatic circle, to allow one's name to be bracketed with those that had gone down in infamy, to keep his head held high through all the bitter innuendo, took courage of a very extraordinary sort, a particularly English kind of madness.

Why should he still have to keep silent? Even if it was only for Johnnie's sake, and the boys', his name should be cleared at last. She half hoped the Fleet Street hawks would be on to it, for she was sure no explanation, no revelation, would be forthcoming from the old man himself. There, at least, she knew she had the size of him. She knew all about pride herself. She was the sort who would not allow anyone to put her down. It was inbred with her strong, independent Scottish nature. It came, she thought, from sorting out moral choices more or less directly with God. A kind of grudging, slow and hesitant admiration for the old man was replacing her anger and dislike – at least, for that part of him that could not be tainted by what people thought.

He hadn't wanted her for Johnnie. Well, that was too bad. He wasn't going to come between them. When – not *if* – Johnnie came back, they would lead their lives as they chose and the old man would have to come to terms with it as best he could. As her own father had had to do, when she had struck the flag for a life of her own. Useless to wish for tenderness from intransigent males who could only relate where they could dominate. That too, was as dead as the dodo.

It was the worst night so far. For twenty-four hours now there had been no news of any sort out of Israel. It could mean the news was too bad to be borne or it could mean delicate negotiations were in the balance and silence was the best means of giving them a chance.

She *knew*, somewhere deep in her psyche, as surely as some of her Gaelic foremothers had claimed for the second sight, that Johnnie was in some dark, airless cell somewhere. It could even be a cave. She knew that there had been pain and degradation inflicted by rifle butt and pistol, that there were bruises on his body, his face. There might have been a gag across his mouth, and a blindfold, and there was certainly thirst of a kind that pushed everything else from the mind.

It was only in the dark and in bed that she permitted tears and she wept now, tears of desperation and panic. At three o'clock, the worst time, the witching hour, she got up and put on the kettle. She sat on a hard chair by the window, praying harder than she had ever prayed in her life before, to the God who was out there in the soft tumescent dawn, letting her know about the joy and wonder of existence in the first mysterious call and trilling note of city birds and the rustling of the wind in city trees.

If it is Thy will, let Johnnie live … I love him, but that doesn't matter … He's a good man with a lot to do … He has children who need him … Let his father say the right thing to his captors … Let him know I am here and praying for him.

Eventually she realised how cold she was. She had scorned a dressing-gown or even slippers. She got back in between the sheets and for a little while she slept, a sweet and dreamless gift of oblivion such as children know, but not for long.

The telephone with its blatant, strident sound shattered her slumbers. She put out a hand and held the receiver insecurely to her ear.

'Helen?'

For a moment she could not identify the voice. 'Who is it?'

'Kenneth. Kenneth Fellowes. Helen, I know it's early but I'm sure you'd want to know. Fowkes and Johnnie have been released. They are on their way home.'

'They are?' Her voice sounded weird, half a scream, half a sob of intense relief. 'Kenneth, how is he? Is he all right?'

'He seems to be. They've been knocked about a bit, but basically he's fine. I have to tell you, though, that Sir Bertram has had some kind of a seizure. They wanted to keep him in hospital in Israel but he's insisted on being flown home. The story's out, Helen – the one I couldn't tell you about. Concerning the old man being a double agent. He's the hero of the hour.'

'Who broke it?'

'Sydney Felder. The Foreign Office did its best to keep the wraps on it, but it seems he got it from the Israelis themselves.'

'I'm glad,' she said. She did not add: for Johnnie and the boys; some deep, inner demand for fair play was satisfied in her and she thought: good old Sydney. It was good Fleet Street had its mavericks who did not always listen to officialdom, with its need, its desire, for smothering secrecy.

'What happened was,' said Kenneth Fellowes, determined she should have as much information as she could take in, 'Fowkes and Johnnie struck off on their own to meet up with these hard-liners. They wanted *all* the facts, you see, not just what was being fed to them by both governments. It was a bit bloody naïve of them, for the result was a secret demand for money, a lot of money. Our government knew if we met the demands, that would be it. Every rebel faction would get in on the act.

'It was amazing, though, how things got moving when Sir Bertram got out there. He'd been a hero of their underground movement in prewar Europe, responsible for saving not hundreds, but thousands, of Jews from the camps. No one broke his alibi or spoiled the front he had put up – that's the truly amazing thing. He had to live with that fudged, ambiguous image, treated like a semi-traitor.'

She was silent, not knowing what to say.

'Helen? Are you there?'

'When are they expected to arrive?'

'About eleven-thirty.'

'I'm going to the airport.'

'They'll have to be de-briefed. It'll be chaos.'

'I'm going, Kenneth,' she reiterated.

Her bedroom looked as though it had been hurricane-struck as she pulled clothes from drawers and wardrobe in a whirl of indecision. It was at once ludicrous and necessary that she should look the best she ever had. She pulled on a white skirt and jacket with a navy blouse. It would have to do. She pulled her hair through a little padded doughnut and arranged it in a chignon as Johnnie liked to see it, adding gold earrings in a circular, plaited design and a gold choker necklace. She could not spend any more time on her looks – there was so much still to arrange.

She had never seen so many photographers in her life. They were behaving like badly brought up children, fighting and squabbling for position in the enclosure near the runway that the authorities had set up for them.

Harvey Bentley detached himself from the group of waiting officials and came over to her, nervously dropping papers as he tried to light a calming cigarette.

'If you would like to come to the waiting-room,' he offered, 'we'll arrange for you to have a few minutes to yourselves before the gannets descend.'

She took up his offer gratefully. Through the waiting-room windows she saw the plane hop almost casually over the airport horizon and taxi into place. She saw Johnnie and Fowkes descend and then a stretcher bearing the old man. It was very difficult to remain where she was, but she waited, knowing that every extra body on the tarmac would only hold things up, put back the moment of reunion.

The doors opened and the plane passengers piled into the anteroom with the waiting officials. Johnnie came straight towards her and put his arms around her. 'Thank God,' he said in her ear. 'Thank God to be back. Are you all right?'

She put a hand up and touched the bruises on his cheek. 'You dope,' she said, 'you idiot.' She could feel his thin, muscular body through the clean, borrowed white shirt and her fingers clutched at him convulsively.

'The children are O.K.,' she said reassuringly. 'Everything is O.K. Now you're home.' She felt some of the tension run out of him. His eyes bored into hers, taking her to that private island of delights that only they knew and shared. And then, only then, their lips met.

'Is Grandpa going to live?'

They had taken the children to see the house in Battersea where they were all going to live, after the wedding in two weeks' time. It was a nice house, a friendly house, with big rooms still filled with the vendor's furniture and a tangly garden where the boys would be able to have a tree house. Now while they rested in the sunny back sitting-room, the boys, in need of their tea, had become languorous and thoughtful. It was Jamie, picking at threads on a tapestry cushion, who put the question.

'He *is* getting better, but it takes a long time, because he is quite old.' Helen smiled at him and drew him to her, smoothing his dark thatch of hair.

What had ailed the old man in Israel had been a stroke. Not a serious one and with physiotherapy he had been promised a good recovery. But he was not a man who took kindly to invalidism and his convalescence had been a shade stormy and unpredictable, to say the least. Helen and Johnnie were going to take the two boys back to their mother, Simonette, to spend these last few days with her before she took off for the States, and then they were scheduled to visit Sir Bertram in the nursing-home.

It was Bertie's turn now to squeeze up beside Helen on the settee. He turned his dark, unsettling gaze – Peter Hart's gaze – on her and said, 'When you marry our father, you won't be our mother, will you?'

She punched him lightly in the stomach. 'You know I won't. I'll be a semi-wicked stepmother. I'll make you eat gruel and sweep out the yard.'

Both boys fell on her now, pummelling her none too gently. 'What's G-R-U-E-L?' demanded Jamie. 'It sounds ugh-y and awful.' 'There isn't a yard!' yelled Bertie. 'So how can I sweep it out?'

'You three are getting too silly for words,' decreed Johnnie. He got to his feet and shooed them in the direction of the car.

When they had deposited the boys, they drove to the nursing-home. These visits were still an ordeal for

Helen, though she did not say this to Johnnie. The old man had not commented on the forthcoming wedding although Johnnie had made a point of talking about the arrangements some point during each visit.

She said, feeling that familiar knot of pre-wedding nerves in her stomach, 'He's not going to accept me, is he? Your father, I mean. The boys I can handle, no problem, but he's going to be different.'

He took his left hand momentarily off the steering-wheel and patted her right one. 'You're a strange animal to him. He doesn't know how to cope with independent women.'

'We're gut enemies,' she said. 'I know that.'

'With one thing in common.'

'What's that?'

'Me.'

They walked along the polished corridor of the nursing-home, with its tasteful vases of flowers and its hospital smell. In the spruce white bed the old man looked pink and frail and was just woken from sleep. Helen smiled at him but did not kiss him. Perhaps she would never do that.

'I see that fella got in,' the old man addressed Helen. 'The one we had all the fuss about. The Labour chap. In the East End.'

'You mean Brendan Cassidy?' Brendan had indeed won the by-election. Two nights ago the papers had carried pictures of him walking towards Westminster and his induction with his new bride, Gita Cohen.

Rose had been at the wedding, but Helen had not been invited. Rose said Gita had forbidden it.

'Brendan will make a good M.P.,' said Helen. 'He's not a narrow man.' She was conscious of Johnnie watching her face and said nothing more. She loved him too much to let him suffer even one jealous pang.

A nurse came in, bearing a cup of Horlicks for the old

man. There was further talk, about Sir Bertram's progress in walking, about when he might be allowed home, about the fact that he would not be well enough to attend the wedding (this last topic aired by Johnnie but unacknowledged by his father).

'Time to go.' Johnnie kissed his father's forehead and Helen wriggled her fingers in farewell. Outside the door, they put their arms about each other's waists as they walked away. In a little, he realised her shoulders were shaking and stopped in alarm. 'Whatever is the matter?' he demanded.

He saw then she was laughing.

'Did you see, the old devil?' she demanded. 'As I left, he *winked* at me. He really did.'

She was walking towards Johnnie. Smiling, intent faces turned towards her: her mother and father, Marie and her brothers, stiff and Scottish and proud in new dear-bought clothes, loving her with their eyes; Rose, managing to look a little shabby even in a brand new coat; the boys, fidgeting in a superhuman effort to be good.

Music, flowers. Her wedding dress was mid-calf, cream brocade, and her mother had brought blue harebells from Scotland to mix in with the hot-house-grown blooms in her hair and her bouquet.

As she came close to him, she gave Johnnie a radiant smile and saw his face light up in response. This was the man she had chosen when she was seventeen and still loved passionately, exclusively, with every instinct and fibre of her being. He only had to cast that look at her, that speaking, eloquent look that talked of need, fervour, certainty, and she was done for, ballads of love poured through her mind and every atom and particle of her danced for joy.

That's where it had begun. In a dance-hall. With the

touch of hands and the fatal, wordless promise of eyes. And oh, my love, my darling, she thought now: I only can dance with you.

Further titles available from Woman's Weekly Fiction

The prices shown below were correct at the time of going to press.